A
SIGNAL
SHOWN

The Wisdom Court Series
Book Two

Yvonne Montgomery

Cover and Book design by eBook Prep
www.ebookprep.com

August, 2014
ISBN: 978-1-61417-648-0

ePublishing Works!
www.epublishingworks.com

DEDICATION

Dedicated to my mother and father.

ACKNOWLEDGMENTS

This book was difficult to write and I am deeply grateful to the people who helped along the way. Margi Evans was a champion beta-reader whose wholehearted response to the work gave me a boost. Carol Caverly pushed me to the ending the book needed when I was ready to stop and cheered me on through the extra effort. Misty Ewegen was a fervent reader who gave me penetrating suggestions and crucial information throughout. Shane Ewegen was meticulous, as always, in finding grammatical and editing issues while urging me on. Love and gratitude to Marlena Gott for "Nightmirrors." Carol Sullivan's critiques of earlier versions of the work helped build the foundation for the completed book. My husband, Bob Ewegen has continued to back my play through all the adventures and I thank him.

To the friends and family members who have maintained interest in this project, thanks so much.

I appreciate the institutional support and member camaraderie of the members of Rocky Mountain Fiction Writers and Colorado Authors League.

Many thanks to Nina Paules and Brian Paules of ePublishing Works. Their excellence in e-formatting, cover design, and marketing have helped reboot my writing career

NIGHTMIRROR

The sidewalk borders a jagged pavement. Old street lamps cast dingy halos into emptiness.

She stumbles and a rock skitters to the gutter. The air reeks of car exhausts and desperation. A noise jerks her gaze to the shadows. Is someone hiding behind the steam from the manhole cover?

Just walk, she tells herself. Just walk. They're waiting for you to come closer.

She clutches the talisman in her pocket, edges sharp against her palm.

Don't search the dark, she tells herself. Keep going, no matter what.

Home abides like a lantern in the nightfall, but the nothings crawl in behind her before the door is shut. She slams the hatch to the cellar. Pulls the shade over the window.

A whisper rouses her. *Don't turn out the lights until you're in bed, and don't let your hands hang over the edge.*

The crooked door creaks open.

The broken doll seeks her out with foreign eyes, doesn't recognize her. Comes for her all the same.

CHAPTER 1

Her own moaning awakened her from the dream.

Brenna Payne rolled toward the nightstand, heard the crumple of paper. Fumbling for the lamp switch, she turned it on and pushed her hair out of her face. From the neighboring pillow, her lover muttered. She thought he'd wake up, but he turned away from the light and she heard the crackle of paper again. Searching the navy coverlet she saw the letter, the one that changed everything, the one prompting them to drink too much wine. Probably the wine had caused the dream, too.

She pulled the single page toward her, started reading again to make sure the words hadn't changed while she'd slept.

Dear Ms. Payne:

It is my great pleasure to inform you that you've been chosen as a recipient of the Wyntham Grant from the Wisdom Court Foundation. The grant is awarded to women scholars and artists who have yet to be recognized for their endeavors.

"I don't even get recognized by my landlord," Brenna muttered.

Your film, STEPS, captivated the Wisdom Court Board of Directors and led to your acceptance. I love this cinematic tour through the twists and byways of places I'd never seen before. I marvel at the peering gargoyle creatures you filmed in what I thought were merely moldings and rainspouts. Your camera angles disoriented me, forcing me to notice fresh landscapes where before I'd seen only buildings and walkways. I am amazed at what you saw and abashed at what I did not— surely the very definition of a work of art. All of us at Wisdom Court hope your movies will be more widely screened.

"From your lips to the Great Projectionist in the sky." Brenna hugged the letter to her nightshirt, giddy at the compliments.

Your living expenses and the support of your work are covered by the grant. Your studio at Wisdom Court will include film-editing facilities, and any supplies you require. The one condition attached to the grant is that you live at Wisdom Court here in Colorado. Family visits and other necessary brief periods away are allowed, of course, but the majority of your year must be spent in Boulder. Our founder, Caldicott Wyntham, believed the exchange of ideas and creative energy among talented women enables a higher level of achievement.

I am sending more complete information about our program. I look forward to hearing from you.

> *Sincerely,*
> *Rose Hertzberg, Director*

"I love you, Rose Hertzberg." Brenna scanned the lines once more, the words of praise glowing like jewels set in gold. *Like rain in the desert, like crocuses in the snow.* "Like chocolate syrup and a maraschino cherry on the double-scoop of life," she whispered. She was on her way at last.

Autumn cast its spell on Colorado's Front Range. Only the tall pines and feathery blue spruce kept their original colors in the wake of cooling nights. Cottonwoods fluttered leaves as bright as pirate dubloons, while the crimson sumac blazed near forsythia foliage wilting on the branches. The pink sandstone slabs of Boulder's Flatirons thrust high against deep blue sky to delay the spill of winter over the Foothills in protection of the three houses nestled at the base of Flagstaff Mountain.

The morning sun warmed the tall stone farmhouse, Wisdom Court's main building. Light beamed through prisms hung at the double windows in Rose Hertzberg's workroom, scattering tiny rainbows across ivory walls. Shelves at one end of the room held fountain supplies, the small-scale pumps, containers of assorted sizes and shapes, and tiny figurines. A collection of stones filled two large bins in one corner.

Rose entered the room slowly. In her mid-fifties, dressed in a blue sweat suit, she moved with the grace of a longtime yoga practitioner. Her curly silver-blonde hair was in a loose knot at her nape, and large gray eyes dominated her fine-boned face. She saw the fountain she'd begun the night before and closed her eyes. "No. Not again."

Three times in two weeks she'd left a work in

progress. Each following morning the rocks and miniatures were reorganized in a circle around the container. After what had happened earlier that summer, the rearranged stones sent chills down Rose's spine.

Was it beginning again?

"Maybe it's the equinox or the phases of the moon," Rose said aloud. "Aura Lee might say that."

"Why would I?" Aura Lee Witherspoon had opened the door after a light tap. "I thought I heard you say to come in, but maybe I imagined it." She was regal in a rustling green caftan, her brass-colored hair braided in a coronet. Tiny gold ankhs dangled from her earlobes, and her blue eyes were twinkling beneath light green eye shadow. She'd long been the Wisdom Court house manager, but Rose saw her as a chatelaine who cared more about the people in her castle than the rooms and furnishings.

Rose moved to block the stone circle from sight, but Aura Lee had already bypassed her and was staring down at the table. She glanced up in curiosity. "Did you arrange the stones around the bowl like this?"

Rose shook her head.

Aura Lee's eyes widened. "Do you know who did?"

Rose hesitated. If Aura Lee perceived even a shred of the supernatural in this, she'd renew her efforts to contact Caldicott. Since the death of Wisdom Court's founder, Aura Lee had conducted rituals and had even forced them into a séance. Despite her failures, she was positive a message from her dearest friend was there, waiting for her to reach it.

"Rose?" Hope shone from Aura Lee's eyes. "Tell me what's going on."

Rose motioned toward the nearby chair for Aura Lee, and sat down. "It started a couple of weeks ago. I've left a fountain unfinished and come back to this, the empty container circled by rocks. I keep the workroom door locked and you're the only other person with a key. Tell me you've been sneaking in."

"As if I would…" Aura Lee's frown faded as she studied the arrangement of stones. "Have you moved anything?"

"This morning? No. But it's been the same, just a single circle. I don't know what it could be or mean."

"A Message from Beyond," breathed Aura Lee. She lifted her radiant face to Rose. "A tear in the veil to the Other Side. This could be the chance I've been looking for."

So much for not leaping to conclusions. "A circle of rocks?" Rose kept her voice gentle.

"Forces are at work here." Aura Lee shivered happily. "Lately I've felt that something major is going to happen." Her eyes kindled with excitement. "I've been watching for signs. And here's a circle, how many times?"

"Three, all told."

"Do you know how powerful that is?"

Rose knew she was about to find out. "Not really."

"A circle can stand for a door between worlds, like I said before. Or it can mean an end, as in all the stages of life, from birth to death. Or it could be a symbol for Circe and her spinning wheel. In Greek myths, she used her spinning wheel to decide the fate of humans."

Rose shrugged impatiently. "How can we interpret something as simple—and, as you point out, as complex—as a circle?"

"Well, of course you have to *figure it out*," Aura Lee sputtered. "Things aren't always easy to get. You've had a circle formed three different times. You *do* know what a big deal the number three is, don't you? You've got the trinity—Father, Son, and Holy

Ghost." She ticked them off on her fingers. "Then there's the mind-body-spirit thing I *know* you've read about. *Third time's the charm*—there's all kind of stuff. The number itself is a powerful symbol, Rose."

Restlessly Rose began moving the rocks back into the bowl, ignoring the small sound of protest from Aura Lee. "I want the forces to leave my fountains alone. Already I come in every morning waiting to see if there's another circle."

Aura Lee was shaking her head in disapproval, her earrings bouncing. "Rose, you have to work with what you get. Somebody's trying to tell you something, and they're using what's available—your rocks."

"So if I left out a pen and paper, I might get a note?"

Aura Lee pushed herself to her feet. "Don't be flippant. The spirits who try to contact us are usually desperate, nothing to joke about. Remember what happened with Andrea."

Rose recalled all too well. When she'd come to Wisdom Court four months before, artist Andrea Bellamy had found herself sketching and painting while in a trance. Only their combined efforts had discovered the causes of that phenomenon.

"I'm hoping Andrea's situation was a one-time occurrence." Rose crossed her fingers unthinkingly. "Finding my fountain rocks arranged in a circle has to have a simple, if crazy, explanation." *What if they're back?*

Aura Lee nodded doubtfully. "Maybe, but you're missing the point. A circle—three separate times—is important. It's reckless to ignore messages, especially from Them."

Rose shuddered, but Aura Lee didn't notice. "I'll start exploring possible meanings. You'll tell me if anything else happens, won't you? If it's Cottie..." Her eyes filled with tears, and she patted her chest, trying to regain control. "It makes me feel so much better to think Cottie's still trying to get through. Promise you'll let me know if there's any other sign?"

"Promise. As long as *you* swear not to cast any spells without telling me. It's only fair that all of us know what's going on."

"Of course." Aura Lee sniffed mightily, her face wreathed in a smile. "I'll get out my divining tools. Maybe I'll be able to pick up emanations from Cottie that way."

"Let me know if you find out something." Rose set the dish of rocks on the shelf above the table.

Aura Lee looked ready to start immediately. "I will. I'll get right on it." She paused, brow wrinkling. "No, first I need to run over to the west house, and then I'll get busy."

Rose glanced at her in question and then remembered. "That's right. Brenna Payne is coming today."

Aura Lee nodded. "I just need to do a double check of the place."

"It'll be good to have her here. I've been missing Dolores and Elizabeth." Dolores Rivera and Elizabeth Schuster had both finished their years at Wisdom Court within the last month. "It's been way too quiet lately."

Aura Lee glanced at the bowl piled with rocks as she headed out of the office. "I don't know about that. There's quiet and then there's just not listening to what's being said." The door clicked shut behind her.

CHAPTER 2

A breeze skittered down Flagstaff Mountain through quivering aspen leaves, brushing across the roses near the courtyard fountain. Rose stumbled on a cobblestone and clutched the clipboard she carried a little closer. Beside her Brenna Payne pulled her sweatshirt hood over her dark hair to stop its swirling about her head. Large brown eyes and black brushstroke eyebrows dominated her heart-shaped face.

Brenna breathed in the clear, chilly air and thought of the L.A. smog she'd left that morning. "Dink would love this," she said aloud.

"Dink?" Rose responded automatically. She glanced at Brenna, but her attention was clearly elsewhere. "Your pet?"

"My boyfriend."

"Oh." Rose hunched a shoulder against another gust of wind. "Hope the name doesn't mean anything anatomical." At the choked sound from Brenna, Rose gasped, "I can't believe I said that!"

Brenna couldn't help but grin. Maybe the woman wasn't as Hitchcock-cool-blonde as she looked. More

Eva Marie Saint in her older years. "It's a dumb nickname, and he's gotten crap for it his whole life. His name's Lucas Dinkland."

Rose cast about for something to say. "Kids can be cruel. And adults, too," she added hastily.

Well, at least she's human, Brenna thought in relief. During her ritual welcome to Wisdom Court, Aura Lee had run through the details, answering the few questions she'd asked. Rose had appeared distracted, if not distant. "No worries."

"Thanks." Rose offered a smile. "I'm not usually so tactless. It's been a strange day." She led Brenna up the rounded steps to the associate house entryway. "Here we are."

Rose held open the door as Brenna entered the hallway, redolent of lemons and floor wax. A dark carpet runner extended to the back wall where two locked postage boxes were set. Brenna's name was on one of them.

"I hope you'll like it here." Rose stopped before the wood door on the left side of the hall, directly across from an identical entrance on the right. Sliding a key into the lock above a shiny brass knob, Rose pushed open the door. "The last associate who lived here, Dolores Rivera, is an artist, a sculptor. We had your film editing equipment installed in the studio she used."

Brenna stepped past her into the living room, her gaze moving swiftly over the leather sofa, the Southwestern art on tawny walls. She dropped her travel bag on the tile floor and assessed what would be her home for the next year. Warm, clean, and inviting. No Tim Burton overtones. So why did she feel a creepy-crawly sensation? She pasted on a smile and tried to inject some enthusiasm into her voice. "I know I'll be able to do good work here."

"I'm sure you will." Rose handed over the key. "This copy is yours. I keep master keys in my office, in case of emergency. The land-line extensions are labeled, and some local pizza places that deliver along with the Chinese place on the Hill are listed on the kitchen phone."

"What else…" Rose paused. "Oh, the new associate who'll share the duplex with you isn't coming yet. She broke her leg and isn't sure when she'll arrive, so you're the sole occupant for now." She added, "Dinner at the main house at seven, drinks beforehand at six-thirty. It's a good way to meet the others, though I'm not sure who'll be there tonight. Tomorrow's Thursday—those are the nights reserved for the group get-togethers, but you're always welcome as long as you let Aura Lee know in advance."

Brenna bit back a yawn. She hadn't slept much the night before, and the airport drill was always a drag. "I'll just veg out tonight, I think. I can meet everyone tomorrow night."

Rose nodded. "I don't blame you. See you when you're ready."

"Sure." Brenna did her best to return the friendly look.

"If you need anything, just yell." Rose smiled a farewell and pulled the door shut behind her.

Brenna closed her eyes for a moment. She was finally here. After she'd received the Wisdom Court acceptance letter, she'd slipped into the zombie zone. That lasted long enough to force her to crank herself into a frenzy to get everything done. The hardest had been getting rid of most of Gran's stuff in the apartment. By comparison, packing up her things and putting them in storage had been simple. It already felt like a dream.

Dreams. Brenna crossed the black and white tiled floor and entered the kitchen. Nightmares had tainted her sleep for months.

"Just need a nap," she said aloud. The sound of her voice startled her. The silence was nearly total, only bird calls to break the calm. *Man, how will I get used to the quiet?* L.A. was loud—car engines, sirens, music from every passing vehicle. Half the reason for A/C was the white noise value.

"I'll make my own noise," Brenna muttered as she turned on the faucet. She found a glass in the cupboard over the sink. She was alone now, not just here in Boulder, but in the world.

Brenna swallowed the water and put the glass on the counter, imagining herself standing on an earth revolving in a cold universe. She let out a shaky breath.

But she wasn't alone. She had Dink. The idea of him, of his hazel eyes under scrunched brows as he played his guitar, of the way he flipped his hair out of his face when he sat at his computer, steadied her. If he were here he'd tell her to get moving, to quit feeling sorry for herself. They'd agreed she had to do the Wisdom Court thing. "Your films deserve to be seen," he'd said the night before. They'd been in bed, clinging to each other as the weight of passing minutes increased. "A year, it's only a year. We'll e-mail like always and Skype. Text and talk on the phone."

Brenna had traced the two wrinkles between his eyebrows with her forefinger, her other hand cupping his strong neck. He'd smelled of spicy soap, and his breath was warm against her cheek.

"I'll be able to fly back every once in a while." Her voice had thickened. "You can come out to Boulder and spend weekends sometimes." He'd nodded wordlessly, eyes sad, and stroked her hair, memorizing the strands with his hands. He'd used the rest of his body to learn her by heart. They'd barely slept at all.

Now Brenna smiled, thinking about Rose's comment about Dink's physical endowments. DiCaprio had nothing on him. It wouldn't be easy to be away from him, and she would miss their lovemaking. But even more important were the feelings he gave her of being loved. Of being understood. Of being part of a whole. She sighed. L.A. was too damned far away.

Brenna returned to the living room for her suitcase and picked up the instruction booklet Rose had left. She walked down the hallway, found the shadowed stairs and went up them to the bedroom. The walls were papered in cool blues, and the large bed had a gray comforter bordered with black vines and maroon roses. The pillows called to her, cloud-fluffy, but she had something to do before she hit the sheets. She swung the case onto the bed and found the Wi-Fi specs she needed. The sooner she got her laptop going, the sooner she could get online. She'd touch base with Dink and find out what was happening in L.A. The connection to her real life was still there. She wasn't alone at all.

Kerry Tomlinson turned the last page of the journal she'd been reading the last two days and closed the top cover, barely resisting an impulse to throw it out the library window. "Dammit, Caldicott, why won't you let me in?" She was silent until she realized that, on some level, she was waiting for an answer. "Oh, balls," she muttered. All she needed was to turn into a crystal gazer like Aura Lee.

Kerry raked her hands through her hair in

frustration. The auburn bob settled back around her cheeks, framing green eyes shadowed by discouragement. She'd been at Wisdom Court for over seven months now and she was no farther along in capturing the real Caldicott Wyntham than the day she'd arrived.

Kerry was drowning in information about the founding of Wisdom Court, reams of it about the various associates over the years. She'd even found profiles of the board members, along with copies of letters nominating future associates, committee reports, and minutes of alumnae group meetings. Caldicott Wyntham was ever present as the force behind the building of the institution, but as a person she was nowhere to be found. With so few glimpses of what had formed her—what had driven her to create Wisdom Court—the biography Kerry struggled to write had no heart.

Nothing about Caldicott's early years: family, education, marital status, or work history as a young woman was to be found. Evidently her life had begun at age thirty-eight in nineteen fifty-nine when she was hired by the Uptide Foundation to expand the donor base for a nation-wide community of professional and amateur ornithologists. Caldicott excelled in her appointed duties and had moved on to greater things after an exemplary run of nearly three years.

"But who *was* she?" Kerry scowled at the volume in front of her. The memory of the old woman who'd welcomed her to Wisdom Court shortly before her death had no warmth now. Kerry had listened to her every word, asking many questions, and Caldicott supplied many answers, along with the fourteen volumes of her journals. But the journals were accounts of Wisdom Court, mostly recollections of its thirty-year history. The few personal details Caldicott gave her hadn't added much about her own developmental years. *We can talk about that later* was a frequent reply. Later had never come.

Kerry recalled Caldicott as she'd been before her sudden final illness. A portrait of her in her thirties hung over the living room fireplace. When Kerry met her, beauty still shone from her older face. Age hadn't affected the strength of her chin or the humor and intelligence in her gray-green eyes. Her flaring eyebrows hinted surprise at what life had thrown at her but she was still willing to see it without blinders. Her hair had faded and thinned, and her neck had wrinkled, but she was still lovely and vital.

"Why didn't I demand more?" Kerry asked aloud. Forget that one didn't demand anything of Caldicott Wyntham. She should have been more assertive. How could one write a biography of someone who wouldn't give up the most basic data? Like where she was born? Who was her family? Were there siblings? Any children? And most of all, what had possessed her to create a foundation dedicated to giving talented women one magical year to reach for the stars? Any biography without that information in it wasn't worth reading, let alone writing.

Kerry jumped at the ring of her cell phone. "Hello?"

Noreen Prescott's deep voice was brusque. "Kerry, I need your help." Kerry pictured the small woman, her hedgehog hair and no-nonsense demeanor. "Any chance of getting you over here for a drink before dinner?"

"Sure." She had no reason to slave away. "What's up?"

"I've just finished the book and I need your younger eyes to glance over the last chapter. I don't see any typos or such, but I've gone over it so many times I wouldn't catch a misspelling of my own name."

Kerry was grinning in delight. Noreen's primary project while at Wisdom Court had been a compilation of quotations from strictly female authors and figures of note. "That's wonderful! Congrats and all that. When will you ship it off?"

"Rose is giving me an agents list." She paused. "I don't suppose you've thought of any who might be interested."

"Yay, Rose. Though you might not need one for a non-fiction work." Kerry had researched whether she would need an agent when Caldicott's biography was completed. *Like that's ever going to happen.*

"I don't know." Noreen added, *"News makes itself known fully only at the moment when it can no longer be forestalled.* Winifred Pennington-Smythe, 1834-1855."

Kerry did the math. "She wasn't very old. What did she do to be worthy of quoting?"

Noreen snorted. "She was an early utopian. One of the more obnoxious I've encountered, too. Every problem dealt with through pure reason, everything measured and arranged just so. Died of a snake bite."

Kerry winced. "Ouch. I'll be there in a few minutes."

Replacing the receiver, Kerry glared at the pile of journals and files on her desk. She would look at Noreen's chapter and have that drink. Maybe five or six. If she couldn't find more information about Caldicott, she might as well drink herself into oblivion.

CHAPTER 3

The old fashioned dining room was fragrant with the spices of Thai food. A bottle of wine graced each end of the long walnut table, one red and one white. Heavy flatware lay on paper napkins along side chopsticks, and serving spoons jutted from large containers of Seafood Pad Thai, Jungle Curry, and rice. Rose had started round the curry from the head of the table as Aura Lee passed a ceramic bowl of green salad from the foot. Judging by the flood of words, nearly all of the room's six inhabitants were talking. Thursday night dinner at Wisdom Court was underway.

Brenna felt as if she'd entered one of the movies she'd watched with her grandmother. A nineteenth century period piece—maybe *Pride and Prejudice*—with gowned ladies and waistcoated men around a table piled with silverware and three or four wineglasses per person. The dining room fostered the image with a built-in sideboard and beveled mirror and a hanging brass light over the table. The chopsticks and only one serviceable stem glass at each place blew the Georgian ambiance. And the women were dressed casually, only two in skirts of any type. No men in waistcoats. Brenna smiled inwardly at the idea of Dink in a waistcoat. The costumes weren't formal, but the conversations here were probably as entertaining as the cat-and-mouse courtship games of Jane Austen's characters.

Brenna had been introduced to the other women, and then they'd all toasted Noreen Prescott, directly across from her, who'd just finished a book of quotations. The tiny woman spoke in a deep, authoritative voice and had a purposeful personality. If she were casting Noreen in a film, Brenna thought, it would be as a judge or politician—definitely a Glenn Close role—who exercised power and knew how to kick butt while she was at it.

Kerry Tomlinson—here Brenna paused. Kerry looked younger than her eyes said she was. She'd be typecast as the Irish lass with that auburn hair and her green eyes, like Janet Munro in *Darby O'Gill and the Little People*. But intelligence came off her in waves. And hurt of some kind, though Kerry did her best to hide it. Maybe the vulnerable best friend would be a better fit for her—the one who always watched out for the main character and complained at her lack of romantic action.

To her left was Andrea Bellamy, a painter, Rose said. She was laughing at a remark by Aura Lee, and her eyes were alight. Chestnut hair framed a lived-in face, friendly and approachable. Brenna thought for a brief moment about how different Andrea looked from so many of the women she saw in L.A., home of cosmetic surgery. Their tight, tanned kitten faces were vacant not only of age, but also of emotion and personality.

"I know you're a filmmaker, but that's about the extent of it," Andrea was saying to Brenna. "What kind of movies do you make?"

"That's what the critics asked." Brenna shrugged, a little embarrassed. "Well, one critic who showed up to one of the two screenings my last film had. He decided on *quirky* and *experimental* and threw in *out-of-the-ordinary world visions*."

"Screw the critics," Andrea said cheerfully. "They're more hung up on their own reactions than what they're reacting to." She smiled over the edge of her wineglass, took a sip. "What are the movies about?"

Brenna felt herself beginning to relax. "My first was a meditation on soffit braces. You know," she added at the confusion on Andrea's face, "those brackets that seem to hold up the undersides of eaves on roofs?" At Andrea's slow nod, Brenna grinned. "I know, it's pretty out-there, but I started noticing them, how many different shapes and designs there are, especially in San Francisco, where I shot most of the film. I love how they're often used to trim a structure, almost as an afterthought, but sometimes they're made with such intricate carving that they just—I don't know—they just shine."

"Like pearl earrings with jeans and a sweatshirt." Andrea smiled.

"Yeah. Not hidden art, exactly, but you have to look for them. I loved doing that piece, though I ended up with a majorly stiff neck." Brenna took a bite of noodles and washed them down with wine. "Then I did *Soul Reflections*, which was a series of window shots. You wouldn't believe how many window styles there are on buildings. And they totally affect the way you see structures."

"You're into architecture, I take it."

"Seriously." Brenna could feel the familiar excitement fill her. "Just think how much we're influenced by our surroundings. City buildings even create their own climate with the shadows they cast and the way they guide wind through the spaces between them. That's how I got interested in the last film I did, *Steps*. I really got into things like stairs and passageways. Oddball walkways, footbridges, stuff like that. People walk in so many different places and I just began *seeing* them, you know? How the various shapes of things dictate the routes people take."

Andrea was nodding in understanding. "Isn't it weird? I mean, when all of a sudden you focus on something you never paid much attention to before. It's like fever vision. Your temp goes up and you get this visual clarity."

"Yeah, that's exactly what it's like." Brenna looked at her with interest.

Andrea sent a glance over the vital faces of the women gathered at the table. "That's one of the cool things about being here at Wisdom Court. Not only do you get to do what you do, you also get to talk about it with a great group of women. I've learned so much more about painting because of the different perspectives I've encountered here."

"It's the exposure to other people's specialties." Kerry had leaned in to listen to Andrea and Brenna. "All of us end up knowing more than when we came here."

"And we get the fun of seeing how projects like Noreen's turn out." Andrea spooned more rice from the circulating carton onto her plate and passed it along to Brenna. "So do you have a new film in mind?"

Brenna passed the rice on to Kerry. "I'm working on a film I call *Signs*, though I'll have to change the title when it's done. M. Night Shyamalan already used it," she said in answer to the question on Andrea's face, "and he's way more famous than me. Anyway, I began paying attention to signs wherever I went. Not the big store marquees or anything like that. I mean the stuff like notices on telephone poles, small sheets of paper in shop windows, the circulars people hand out. I actually saw a man with a sandwich board sign. Then all the papers shoved under windshields, and the messages on ticket stubs. Papers blowing in the wind until someone picks them up. Fortune cookies, papers stuck in library books. Newspaper inserts. You get the drift. All these messages aimed at people, though most of them go unnoticed. So I started photographing them. Early on I used a still camera, then I decided to go back to my sixteen millimeter. I have cans of film—couldn't afford to develop it before now—and I don't even remember what all I've shot. So it'll be an adventure just to see what I've got."

Kerry nodded. "It sounds interesting. So you're not into digital technology?"

"Sometimes, but I'm a sucker for film—you get a better picture quality, and the colors are truer. Digital's easier, cheaper, but I figure with the support I'm getting here, I can afford to do what I really want." Brenna remembered that Kerry had talked about a biography of the woman behind Wisdom Court. "So your thing is writing?"

"Yeah. Though research is the real turn-on." Kerry's face dimmed. "At least that's what I keep telling myself." Brenna raised a brow and Kerry grimaced. "I'm having a hard time with the project right now. Not enough data, so not much writing."

"That's tough." Brenna sympathized for a moment, wondering what she would do if she couldn't find the kinds of images she wanted to photograph. She pushed away the notion with mental crossed-fingers for luck.

"I'm sure Cottie meant to give you what you need." At the end of the table Aura Lee looked both worried and defensive. "I know she wanted you to write the whole story."

"I thought she did...she acted like she did." Kerry sighed in frustration. "I just can't figure out why she would've set me up to fail. It's a lot of trouble for what's basically a nasty practical joke. She didn't come across as that kind of person."

"Well of course not!" Aura Lee's agitation set her long beaded earrings into motion. "She'd never have agreed to the biography if she hadn't intended to go through with it. Cottie wouldn't have made it difficult on purpose."

"We know that," Rose said gently. She rolled the stem of her wine glass between her hands. "She was ill and didn't have the energy to make sure everything Kerry needed was available. She just ran out of time, Aura Lee."

Brenna glanced between the two of them, confused at the intensity of the conversation. "Who's Cottie?" she murmured to Andrea.

"Caldicott Wyntham," Andrea responded in a low voice. "The founder of this place. She died four months ago. Cottie was her nickname. Kerry's project for her year here is to write Caldicott's biography, but she hasn't found a lot of the personal papers and things she needs to wrap it up."

"You're positive you've looked everywhere?" Noreen was asking Kerry. "This house has so many nooks and crannies, you never know where something might be squirreled away."

"How many times have you all helped me look?" Kerry pushed her plate aside. "We've explored every cranny and nook in the place. As for squirrels...who the hell knows?" She slammed her palm onto the table. "The thing that gets me is not knowing why. Why the big mystery? Why the total blank about her early life? I can't even figure out where she was born." Her green eyes snapped with exasperation. "I think she was running away from something."

"Just a minute," Aura Lee exclaimed. "Just a cotton-picking minute." Her face flushed with temper. "You may be frustrated, but that's no reason to slander Cottie."

"It's not slander, I'm only saying it's weird to have so much information hidden. Come on, Aura Lee," Kerry challenged. "Even you don't know any of that stuff, and you were her best friend. What in the sweet hell was she trying to cover up?"

The absence of noise woke Brenna, and she rolled over to look at the clock on the nightstand. One thirty-six. She groaned and burrowed under the blankets, hoping she could ease back into sleep. Her mind started replaying the events of the day, lingering on the shifting moods displayed at dinner.

She had to sympathize with Kerry. What a drag, to be hired to write a biography, then not be given the materials she needed to get the job done. Of course, if Caldicott Wyntham had been really sick, she couldn't be blamed for screwing up. But blame didn't matter. It had to be a writer's worst nightmare.

Unbidden, the image of her grandmother slipped into her mind. How many nights had Gran wandered down the hallway, face twisted with fear as she peered into each room, searching for something familiar? Then her features would almost relax as Brenna came to lead her back to her room. But her uncertain smile couldn't offset the desolation in her eyes.

Okay, enough of that. Brenna threw off the covers and grabbed her sweatshirt from the chair by the window. She headed out toward the stairs and padded down them, making for the kitchen. A glass of milk might help.

The refrigerator light was bright, but when the door closed, the dark pushed against the kitchen windows. During the day, the uncovered panes let the outer world inside, but now the night waited. Brenna poured the milk, and returned the carton to the shelf on the door. She turned her back on the windows and carried the glass into the study, where the shutters blocked the dark. As she slid into the desk chair she turned on the laptop and in a matter of moments was online.

Dink, I'm feeling shaky about this whole thing. The women here are great, into happening stuff and willing to talk about it. They act interested in what I'm doing, too, but I don't know anybody yet, so I feel totally out of it. They're smart and talented. I'm feeling like I'm not. Brenna paused, letting her wrists rest on the desk. Did she sound like a total loser? Dink wanted to know everything, wanted to be supportive, but how would it be for him to learn about things he couldn't change?

You asked about the dreams, she typed. They'd promised to keep it real, to be honest with each other. *They're still with me, damn them. Twice last night I sat up in bed, convinced I'd just heard Gran call me. It's freaky, because it's so quiet at night here. Hardly any sound at all except for the wind now and then. I'm alone in this building. I told you about the woman who'll be living on the other side of the duplex—when she gets here—she has a broken leg—so if I hear anything, it trips me out cuz I know nobody's there. Hope she heals fast.*

After that there wasn't much to say. She kept hoping he'd respond with an Instant Message, but he didn't. Brenna sent her love and signed off. Dink was probably asleep, or maybe he'd gone out. She turned her mind away from the image of him at a club, dancing with someone else.

Brenna paused at the doorway of the study and went back for her laptop. She passed through the living room and headed back upstairs. What did she need? Comfort movie or an action flick? *Casablanca* or the last James Bond? Couldn't think too much with chases and battles. She paused, thinking *Last of the Mohicans*. Daniel Day-Lewis was way too buff, though, and the love scenes way too yummy. She leaned against the pillow and entered another title. *Speed* would do the trick. Mindless bus travel: the complete cure for a troubled mind.

Soon Brenna was focused on Keanu Reeves and Sandra Bullock coping with the downsides of public transportation. She drank more milk, and kept her mind blank, refusing to allow any toxic memories to surface. Over the last few years she'd found ignoring what couldn't be changed was better than fighting shadows.

It was hours before she was able to fall asleep once more. And then she dreamed.

NIGHTMIRROR

Trees whisper outside, leaves rustling on palsied limbs. Night sneaks in, stealing the light, leaving the forms in the room gray and still.

She sleeps shallowly, her body cold, fear colder. She can't wake up. Sleep is a crouching beast, fiercely holding her down.

But the door is unlocked. Lock the door.

The air thickens as minutes ooze by and something waits to get in, waits to strike.

The pillow hardens and her heart slams in her chest. Lock-lock. Lock-lock.

LOCK THE FUCKING DOOR

The gate shrieks open and the night cracks open and the banshee is free, shroud twisting.

It floats to the bed, it hovers beside her, grotesque fingers reaching for her.

She can't move.

It's moaning, keening. The empty eyes have hell inside.

Who are you? Who are you? She doesn't know.

She's so small…smaller yet…not seen…not known. She's gone.

CHAPTER 4

The upstairs hallway of the stone farmhouse was hazy in the afternoon sun. The air was scented with lemons and furniture wax and traces of cinnamon. The bedroom doors were shut, making the corridor feel long and narrow.

"So, what're we hunting for?" Rose asked Kerry. She'd been working on her fountains, casual in jeans and a blue sweater, and she had a smudge of dirt on one cheek.

"The usual." Kerry's gaze skimmed over yards of wood trim, pausing at occasional bumps in the wallpaper. "Noreen got me going again with her comment about nooks and crannies. I can't shake the feeling something's here. A little hidey-hole or concealed panel, you know?"

"Yeah. But we've looked everywhere." Rose started down the hall, Kerry trailing behind. "I can't imagine Caldicott scooping out a hole, stuffing in her private papers and wallpapering over it. Too much trouble, and hell to access."

"It sounds crazy." Kerry turned, casting a calculating eye over the space. "I'm obsessed with the idea of wall safes or hidden compartments. What haunts me is the feeling that it's at my fingertips, just waiting to be discovered."

Rose's smile was doubtful. "Why didn't Caldicott tell one of us where this mythical hiding place is? She arranged for you to come here to write about her life, and if she'd had any deep, dark secrets, she would've told you about them, right?" She started down the back stairs, but Kerry stopped her with a hand on her shoulder.

"Let's look in her room."

"Again?" Rose glanced at her face and turned back. She led her down the hall and opened the third door.

Caldicott might have stepped out of the bedroom moments before. It was the same as always with wheat-colored walls, white-enameled crown molding, the Oriental carpet swirling with reds and greens and golds. The large walnut bed, with its airy canopy of pale green silk, had plumped pillows and a patterned throw draped over the end of the flowered duvet.

Kerry's gaze went to the walnut armchair and the chaise longue in front of the double window. There, a little over four months ago, they'd talked about the biography, Caldicott reclining on the chaise, the throw protecting her from any chill. Kerry had loved sitting in the curving chair, now and then glancing at their images in the round mirror above the small gas fireplace. She'd imagined their reflected forms as a portrait of the connection between them, framed by the gilded vines around the beveled glass.

She fought against sadness. "I can almost feel her here."

Rose ran her fingertips across the top of the chest of drawers beside the door. "That's why we haven't packed up everything yet. Aura Lee still comes in here sometimes just to sit. Neither one of us can bear to clear it out."

"We went through the drawers, and the closet." Kerry's gaze landed on the blanket chest at the end of the bed. "Maybe a false bottom?"

Rose shrugged. "Check it out."

Five minutes of poking around and measuring produced nothing from the old chest. Kerry went to the small secretary against one wall. "I've looked here." Still, she pulled down the writing surface and opened the tiny drawers. "Nothing." Under her grief simmered anger and a sense of betrayal.

Rose got up from the chair. "Let's go have some coffee. Unless I'm hallucinating, Aura Lee's been baking."

"Okay." Kerry trailed behind her down the stairs. At the bottom step, a russet dachshund stared up at them, tail wagging.

"Strudel, sweet girl." Kerry bent to pet the little dog and then followed Rose into the kitchen, breathing in the perfume of cinnamon rolls. Strudel trailed after them. "This dog might lobby us for some baked goods." Strudel barked and sat down, waiting to be served.

"You think?" Rose glanced about swiftly, and tore a tiny piece of roll from the pan. "Don't tell Aura Lee." She held out the morsel and the dachshund took it with a quick lick of her tongue. "Strudel and I have a deal: she lets me rub her belly and I pay her off for the privilege."

Kerry smiled. "How did you first meet Caldicott?"

"At a yoga class at the rec center." Rose thought for a moment. "It would've been about twelve years ago. You want coffee?"

"Please. I'll get the rolls." Kerry used her finger to scoop a bit of icing from the edge of the pan and tasted it. "Mmmm, sin and degradation on a plate."

Putting the rolls on saucers, she carried them to the table. "I didn't know Caldicott ever studied yoga."

Rose filled two cups with coffee. "I think she'd been practicing for years, maybe decades, by the time we met." Her smile was reminiscent. "I don't know why she'd signed up for a basic class, but there she was, and there I was, and we hit it off. Grab the cream out of the fridge, will you?"

Kerry picked up the sugar bowl as well. They pulled chairs out from the table and sat down. Strudel curled into a ball at Rose's feet, watching keenly for spills.

"So what were you doing when you weren't studying yoga?" Kerry took a bite of roll and closed her eyes at the blend of butter, cinnamon, and lemon on her tongue.

Rose glanced at her with a wry expression. "I was a professional wife. My husband required a lot of support for his brilliant career, and I provided it." She reached for the cut glass cream pitcher.

Kerry wondered at the edge of bitterness in her voice. "Sorry if I struck a nerve."

"How could you know about my nerves? Or anybody else's?" Rose sipped her coffee and put the cup down with a sigh. "Sorry. I don't know why I turn into an ice queen every time I think about who I was back then."

"What happened?"

Rose shook her head. "I got married when I was twenty, at the end of my sophomore year of college. Jim had just graduated, and was accepted at CU for a master's in business. So we got married and moved to Boulder. The plan was for me to finish my degree here. Of course I got pregnant almost immediately. I settled down to building our nest and waited for the baby." She added in a lower voice, "I had a miscarriage." She tore a piece off her cinnamon roll.

"Oh, Rose. I'm so sorry."

Her eyes were sad. "Thank you. It was a long time ago, but it still hurts." She took a deep breath. "We tried again after about six months. I'd lost any desire to go back to school. Couldn't see what difference it would make." She studied her hands for a moment. "I had two more miscarriages over the next couple of years. Jim finished his master's degree and got a job in Denver. We'd bought a house here in Boulder and I set out to make it a showplace to advance his career."

Kerry leaned back in her chair. "You didn't get a job?"

Rose's laugh was short and bitter. "Certainly not. Jim didn't want anyone to think he wasn't able to support us. I donated time to the hospital guild, that sort of thing. I learned a lot over the years, in some ways more than I might have in a paying job. Jim was climbing the corporate ladder at Mountain Bell, and I gave dinner parties and volunteered with the various charities his company sponsored."

"So what went wrong?" Kerry asked softly.

Rose's mouth twisted. "It's such a cliché. Jim had an affair with his secretary. She got pregnant. That was final proof that it was my uterus, not his prick. Jim had to do the honorable thing, right? So he asked for a divorce, paid me off, and became a doting father at last."

Kerry fought back a desire to badmouth the absent Jim. "And you?"

Rose's shoulders drooped. "I came damned close to becoming an alcoholic. Here I was, forty years old, dumped for a younger woman, a fertile one at that. But after a while I realized I didn't want to be a drunk. I started some classes, core curriculum stuff to jumpstart a shot at a bachelor's degree. I thought I might teach, something like that. And I decided to try yoga, since it was something totally different." Her smile grew, became genuine. "I met Caldicott, and it felt like we'd known each other forever. After I graduated she hired me to help her here, and that led to the job as co-director for the five years before she died."

Rose pushed back her chair to get them both more coffee. "The board made me director after Caldicott died, as you know. And here we are."

"Aren't we just. I wish I'd asked you before now." Kerry shrugged at her quizzical glance. "I mean about your life, not just stuff about Caldicott. I've been on such a tear with the biography…I'm sorry you had such a rough time."

"Sweetie, we all have a rough time, sooner or later. Caldicott was an angel for me. I just hope I'm doing the kind of job here that she thought I could do." *And that I can handle the haunted house stuff.* Rose wondered if Aura Lee had communed with any spirits yet.

"You know she'd be pleased."

The doorbell rang from the front of the house and Strudel trotted toward the sound. "Aura Lee can get it." Rose took another bite of her cinnamon roll.

"I never asked you before—I guess I figured you'd tell me if there was anything I needed to know—but I've wondered about when Caldicott died." Kerry paused, uneasy at the feeling she was trespassing on private emotional territory.

Understanding filled Rose's eyes. "You want to know if she said anything before she died. About her papers."

Kerry nodded, feeling small. "I'm running out of ideas. I've written about the Wisdom Court years and I've interviewed every pertinent person. Without earlier information, I can't take the biography any further."

"No harm done." Rose set her cup on the table, lined it up with an invisible marker. "Aura Lee and I were with her, and the doctor—Jerri—was there, too. Caldicott was in and out of consciousness." Rose's voice thickened. "She thanked me and Aura Lee." She took a breath and let it out. "I held her hand and she dozed a while. Then, at the end, she squeezed my hand, really hard. She opened her eyes and said, *All in bad time, Rose.* And she died."

Kerry thought a moment. "I've heard that before. *All in bad time.* Where have I heard that?"

Rose wiped at tears with a napkin. "Something was on her mind, but that's all she said."

"Something on her mind. I wish I knew what." Kerry swallowed at the lump in her throat. If only she'd been there to hear for herself. She glanced up, saw the sympathy in Rose's eyes. "I appreciate your telling me about it. I'll just keep looking for more 'til my time here runs out. I have four months left. However it goes, this year has meant so much to me."

"Oh, Kerry," murmured Rose. "I wish I could remember something, anything that might—"

Aura Lee appeared at the kitchen door. Her eyes were dark with trouble. "Rose, come with me, please. We've got a situation." She turned without another word and went back the way she'd come.

Rose and Kerry got to their feet and hurried after her.

In the quiet kitchen the cups and plates on the table moved slowly to form a circle.

CHAPTER 5

The autumn sun slid behind the Flatirons, no clouds to break its fall. As the windows darkened, shadows reached toward the wingback chairs in front of the fireplace. There a man stood motionless, his attention on the portrait of Caldicott Wyntham above the mantel.

Rose and Kerry walked across the room, behind them Aura Lee pausing to switch on the two floor lamps along the way. In the sudden light, the man turned toward them. He appeared to be in his mid-to-late thirties, of medium height and frame. Casual in slacks and a suede jacket, his stance was rigid, maybe braced for something unpleasant, Kerry thought. Light brown hair brushed brows bent in a frown over narrowed blue eyes. At his feet a worn leather briefcase leaned against the hearthstone.

"This is Maxwell Steadman," Aura Lee said. "He claims Cottie hired him last year to research a woman called—" She looked him. "I've forgotten her name."

"Clara Trinder. Ms. Wyntham wrote me to ask for a genealogical background for the woman, as well as any information I could find regarding her whereabouts." His clipped British accent emphasized his impatience. "Some family connection she hoped to write a book about, I believe."

"You're a genealogist?" Rose sank into a chair as Kerry moved past her. Aura Lee perched on the sofa, face creased in bewilderment.

"I am an historian, but genealogy forms a good deal of my professional research at the moment." He shifted his weight and tensed momentarily.

Something didn't feel right. Kerry searched his face for signs of deceit. "I haven't found anything about that in Caldicott's records. Where in hell did you spring from?"

Maxwell Steadman raised one eyebrow, letting the silence grow until Kerry could feel her cheeks heat. "I suppose I could answer any number of ways," he said with soft precision. "From the mind of Zeus, from the dreams of angels, from the deep blue sea. Or even the more boring: from the usual source."

"Cottie never said a word about this," Aura Lee murmured, worried. "And surely she would have." Strudel had jumped up beside her and she patted the dog absently.

Steadman shrugged, his mouth tightening. "You've gone through her papers?" At Rose's nod he added, "Evidently she didn't want to share the information. It's not unheard of."

Kerry heard scorn in his voice. "We're not being nosy. Rose worked closely with Caldicott, and Aura Lee was her oldest friend. She had every reason to tell us about such a project, but she didn't."

He surveyed her without expression. "And you are?"

"Kerry Tomlinson. Caldicott Wyntham's biographer."

Rose leaned forward. "Forgive our lack of manners,

Mr. Steadman. I'm Rose Hertzberg, director of Wisdom Court. And you've met Aura Lee." She slanted a look at Kerry. "I think I might have come across something about this in Caldicott's mail shortly after she died."

"You're kidding." Kerry frowned, too aware of Steadman's cynical gaze. "Why didn't you say something?"

"Things were kind of busy."

Steadman glanced between the two of them. "I had to suspend my activities for a few months, and my secretary sent out notices to my clients. You should have received one here."

"Please sit down, Mr. Steadman." Rose gestured to a chair. "At least let's be comfortable while we talk."

He bent to retrieve the briefcase at his feet. In the time it took for him to come round the cocktail table to seat himself on the other wingback chair, Kerry noticed both a limp and that he moved with natural grace despite it.

"I suppose I should have apprised you of my impending arrival." The chill in Steadman's voice deepened. "However, circumstances worked against me." His glance went once more to the portrait over the fireplace. "I take it that she is Caldicott Wyntham."

"When she was younger." Aura Lee's eyes misted as she looked up at the painting. "She was a great woman. We won't see the like of her any time soon." Beside her, Strudel was whining softly, her tail moving slowly back and forth.

"Of course." Aura Lee stiffened at the arid note in Steadman's voice and Kerry studied him with sharpened attention. "I'm sure she was extraordinary," he added swiftly. "I have little to go on, not having met her, but one who arouses such loyalty in her friends is assuredly a very special person."

What a puffed-up twerp, Kerry thought, nose wrinkling.

Strudel jumped to the floor and trotted to Steadman's chair. In an instant, she'd leapt onto the seat cushion and crawled into his lap. He gazed down at her in surprise.

"Strudel!" Aura Lee half rose from the sofa. "I'm so sorry, Mr. Steadman. Here, give her to me. I can't imagine why she did that. She's usually wary of strangers."

"It's all right." Steadman looked down at the little dachshund. "I like dogs." His long fingers apparently found the perfect spot behind one of Strudel's ears, for she closed her eyes in bliss, dropping her chin to his leg.

"Incredible." Rose looked at him in amazement.

"I do hope," Steadman went on, still stroking the russet fur, "you'll work with me as I endeavor to finish the job Ms. Wyntham hired me to do."

"Why?" Kerry didn't trust him an inch, no matter what Strudel thought.

"Several reasons, Ms. Tomlinson." For the first time, he smiled, and Kerry's breath caught at the change it made in his face. The remote expression he'd worn melted, revealing charm, even humor. "First, I was hired to find out the history of the Trinder woman, and I finish the jobs I take on. Second, in my research I found some gaps in information which can only be filled from this end of the process."

Rose's return smile held little warmth. "We need to do several things before we launch into any exchanges of information. May I see some identification?"

"What?" He seemed taken aback, but as Rose began to speak again, he stopped her with a raised hand.

"No, it's completely reasonable. I assure you I am merely completing the job I began some six months ago." He pulled a narrow leather billfold from a breast pocket of his jacket and removed a folder from it. "My passport," he murmured as he held it out to Rose. "I have other bona fides if you'd like to see them."

I'm sure you do, Kerry thought. Probably a driver's license for your Rolls and a monogram on your knickers.

He reached to his briefcase, holding Strudel with his other hand to keep her steady. After fishing around, he pulled out an envelope. "Here's a copy of the inquiry from Ms. Wyntham." He passed it to Rose and settled the dog more firmly on his lap.

Rose examined the passport and letter, glancing up at him when she'd finished. "May I make copies of these?" At his nod, she handed them to Kerry. "Thank you, Mr. Steadman. It all seems to be in order." Her face was shuttered.

"Please, call me Max. Now, might you tell me why you are so hesitant about this situation?"

Rose shook her head. "In this day and age, you shouldn't have to ask. What with identity theft and the various other activities we're all warned against, I admit to feeling uneasy under the circumstances. I need to confirm the paper trail of your dealings with Caldicott, given she has died. Frankly, I'm not sure there's any purpose to continuing your investigations."

"Well." Max let out a breath. "We're at cross purposes, then, aren't we? How can we get beyond them?"

Rose got gracefully to her feet. "First I need to talk to my board of directors, as well as with the Wisdom Court attorney. Then, based on their reaction to your proposal, we'll proceed to the next step. Do you have a card I can show them?"

"Certainly." Steadman had risen from his chair, carefully setting Strudel on the cushion. He slid a business card from one pocket and handed it to her, then bent to retrieve his briefcase. "I'm staying at the University Inn, room two-twelve. Have you any estimate how long this vetting process will take?"

"I'll be calling the various people involved first thing tomorrow." Rose extended her hand and he clasped it. "I'll be in touch as soon as I've spoken with them. Kerry, will you show Mr. Steadman out after you've made copies of his documents?"

"Glad to." Kerry rose to her feet.

"Thank you, Mr. Steadman—" At the glance he shot her, Rose substituted, "Max. I'll contact you soon."

Easing around Strudel, who'd jumped from the chair, clearly ready to accompany them, Kerry led the way to the library and the copier in the corner. She motioned to a chair. "Make yourself comfortable. This'll only take a moment."

"I'll stand, thanks." At his feet Strudel barked sharply, and, puzzled, he bent to pat her head. "What's the matter, girl?" he asked softly. Strudel panted at him with a canine grin and rolled onto her back to allow him to scratch her belly.

You dachshund slut, Kerry thought in wonder. Strudel certainly had no doubts about Max Steadman.

She copied the documents, all the while listening to Max croon nonsense to the enamored dog. Another minute or two and I'll be panting, too, she thought wryly. Nothing like a little sweet talk from a man with a British accent.

"Well, I think that takes care of it." Kerry straightened the pages and cast him a glance. He stood straight, his face assuming its noncommittal mask. "Let me see you to the door." She started out of the library.

"As long as you prevent it from hitting me on the backside on the way out," he muttered from behind her.

Kerry stopped abruptly and turned to face him. "Excuse me?"

"Forgive me." His tone was as wooden as his expression. "I must be more jetlagged than I thought." At her steady regard, Max added stiffly, "I was hoping to complete my research quickly. This delay is…irksome."

Welcome to the NFL. Kerry led him toward the front door. "You can hardly expect us to let you go through Caldicott's records without checking you out first."

"Of course not." She swung open the door and he paused. "I hope Ms. Hertzberg will contact me soon."

"She said she would." Kerry waited with impatience for him to leave. "She tends to keep her word."

"Very well, then." He nodded to her and walked down the steps, his limp more pronounced than before. Strudel barked twice, sharply, but he didn't turn back.

Kerry closed the door, just managing to avoid slamming it. What a pompous prig, lacking only the proverbial three-piece suit and a bowler to completely fulfill the stereotype of the London twit. But he liked dogs. Very good-looking, too, whispered her hormones.

"Shut up, hormones," Kerry muttered as she reentered the living room. Attractive the man might be, but his appearance was as disturbing as the serpent's arrival in Eden. He knew things about Caldicott she'd been unable to find. How much more such information did he have? And how could she get her hands on it?

Rose and Aura Lee watched as she approached

them, Strudel trotting behind her.

"What did you say, dear?" Aura Lee asked.

"Nothing." Kerry flopped onto the sofa. "Can you believe that guy? What can this be about?" She appealed to Rose. "Did you really find a reference to the project he was talking about?"

Rose nodded. "As I recall, it was a note to the effect that there'd been a delay of some sort. I didn't pay much attention because I didn't have time to look for the original correspondence that day. Then, with the funeral arrangements and all, I forgot about it. I finally recognized his name, though. I'll find the note before I call the board members."

Aura Lee shifted as Strudel jumped up beside her. "Cottie never said a word about writing a book. And," she added miserably, "in all the years I knew her, she never mentioned her family. I don't understand why she would have gone to a stranger for something like that." Her normal vitality had ebbed. Even her brassy hair looked dimmer.

Kerry was swept with a powerful and unexpected urge to protect Aura Lee, to somehow shield her from any information about Caldicott that might await them. If she felt a pang at not knowing about the project Steadman described, how much more upsetting was it for Aura Lee to realize her closest friendship held secrets?

She felt a shiver down her back. Oh, stop it, she thought irritably. So Caldicott had planned a book. Big deal. She herself hadn't found anything about it because she hadn't been able to find Caldicott's freaking papers. Maybe Max Steadman would be the key to discovering all of the aspects of Caldicott's earlier life.

"I'd better get things together so I can call the board members in the morning," Rose said, getting to her feet. "Mustn't keep Mr. Steadman waiting, right?" Her faux British accent was dead-on.

"That's *Max*, dear," Aura Lee murmured. She pushed herself out of her chair, moving slowly, looking older than she had earlier in the day. Strudel followed at her heels.

Kerry watched them head toward the kitchen, that strange sense of disquiet stealing through her once more.

NIGHTMIRROR

She creeps across the broken boards, keeping away from gaps where hell is glimpsed below.

The stairs drip with blood, and she clutches worn rails, bracing not to skid, not to fall.

Feeling the stares from the shadows, she keeps her gaze ahead, loath to see the fingers through the grates.

Moaning seeps through fetid air and she prays it stops.

A Keeper comes all dressed in white, cloying smile under measuring eyes.

She hears the cry. *Don't leave me here.*

But the dosages are monitored, says the voice beside her, and periods of distress are short.

When you return next week, the voice repeats, you'll see improvement. When you return next week...

Next week and...

Next week and...

She creeps across the broken boards, greater gaps where hell is glimpsed below.

(Run for your life)

CHAPTER 6

Rose crossed the last name off her list. The Wisdom Court board of directors had been notified of Max Steadman's appearance at the house, and of his request to pursue the job Caldicott had evidently hired him to do. Marjorie Hollenbeck, the counsel for the board, would get back to her. And then we can deal further with the confident Mr. Steadman, Rose thought.

With a glance at her watch, she decided to steal an hour to work on her latest fountain. She'd found a miniature bridge and in her mind's eye she saw it set among the rocks she'd arranged as a mountain landscape. She might put a tiny house on a taller stone, implying a road on either side of the bridge. It would suggest an inhabitant who could hear the bubbling water.

Rose unlocked her workroom door and went in, switching on the overhead lights. She glanced at the fountain on the table. The stones she'd chosen—a geode, milky and rose quartz, and several jagged pieces of feldspar found on the hillside above Chautauqua Park—were arranged in a circle around the empty bowl.

"Damn," she whispered. She looked around the room but nothing else was out of place, and a wave of anger overcame her. "What do you want?" she cried. "Why do you keep doing this?"

Why would someone take apart her fountains, and only the unfinished ones at that? None of them were ruined, and she'd had no trouble recreating them. To remove the rocks, to arrange them in a circle…it was weird enough to bother her. Who was doing this over and over again?

She settled heavily onto her chair. "Stop trying to fool yourself," she whispered. It made more sense to admit to a paranormal explanation than to pretend a madman was repeatedly breaking into Wisdom Court to dismantle her table fountains. *The rational explanation is that we have a haunting here.*

Aura Lee would be so excited at her acceptance of the supernatural. She would redouble her efforts to contact the troubled spirits trying to communicate with them.

Rose considered the board members with whom she'd just spoken, and her ongoing efforts to achieve a balance between the imaginative and pragmatic energies among them. *I bet they'd love to hear my conclusion about this problem.*

She tugged open the drawer where she kept miniatures to use in the fountains. Pulling out the small bridge, she examined the delicate arch. She'd long thought that bridges didn't always have an easy time of it since the conditions at either end could be contradictory. She'd compared herself to a bridge more than once, with Aura Lee on one side, determined to reach Caldicott beyond death. At the other end were the Wisdom Court associates, the board, and the so-called real world. Rose looked again at the ring of stones on the table. Now she was recognizing a third group, the entities behind the odd events at Wisdom Court. "A new constituency," she said softly. Stuck in the middle, she thought, surrounded by all the players.

The familiar whir of the sixteen-millimeter projector lifted Brenna's heart. It was a sound she'd heard too rarely over the past year. Even the heat from the bulb casting images onto the screen was a source of comfort. She let out her breath in a long sigh. She could work again.

The first batch of developed film had arrived that morning, delivered by Raymond, a stocky man with a gap-toothed smile and a gray ponytail. He'd cracked jokes while she signed for the containers and then had left to continue on his rounds, tapping the horn of his van in farewell as he pulled out of the gate.

Now, settling into her padded chair, Brenna adjusted her earphones and switched on the iPod. To the intricate music of The Fifth Utility, she watched in cautious anticipation as the first reel unwound its contents. The beginning was a long shot of a telephone pole jacketed with papers taped and stapled over its rough surface. The focus tightened to a rectangular flier edged with a wavy line.

PLACEBO EFFECT
Laguna Hall
July 23, 8 p.m. Doors Open
$8 or $4 with canned food donation to the
Southside Food bank

Brenna remembered filming the notice because of the band's name. She'd loved the idea of a cure-all rock show, the sign sparking a bit of cheer during a sad time. The image on the screen faded into black, and then a pig crudely cut from plywood appeared. On its vividly yellow side was painted a clock face with round lashed eyes and a grinning mouth. Under it was scrawled:

RIBS BY SYB
All U CAN EAT IN ONE HOUR

The idea of timed gluttony had tickled her fancy, and she'd imagined a woman standing over her customers with a stopwatch. Did she snatch the plates away when time was up?

The next clip had a mural painted on a brick wall in an alley off Ventura Boulevard. It was of a small adobe pueblo in a night cityscape with stylized skyscrapers looming over it. Purple shadows extended across the flat roof and the ends of the support timbers cast cylindrical shapes along the wall. In one square window a candle shone light into the darkness. No words, no human figures, just the image of a simple structure in a complex world. Brenna had never found out whether the painted work was graffiti or had been commissioned. The image had evoked both delight and a sorrow she didn't understand. As she viewed it again, she was grateful to have recorded it on film.

The cell phone in Brenna's pocket vibrated twice. She slid it out, and saw the call was from Dink, the third one that day. She flipped open the phone as she pulled out her earbuds. "Hi, babe. How's it going?" She reached to turn off the projector.

"Okay. Just need to hear your voice again."

Dink sounded tinny and far away but the idea of him flooded into her mind. Brenna's fingertips tingled with the desire to trace his tanned neck, to comb through his curly brown hair. She yearned to feel his skin next to her own. "Well," she started, but the sudden lump in her throat made her stop until she could take a breath. "I'm still here." She rubbed a finger against one eyebrow. "What're you doing?"

"Writing a crappy song." Fatigue roughened his voice. "So far the words and the melody don't get along. And the bridge is for shit. How about you?"

"Reeling film. Just got my first lot from the lab. It's good to see some of these things again."

Dink didn't say anything for a minute, but the silence was heavy with unspoken thoughts. Just as Brenna started to fill the gap, he muttered, "I miss you."

"Oh, yeah, me, too." Longing made it hard to breathe. Brenna shut her eyes. "It's only been a few days."

"That's what's got me going. A whole *year*, Bren." His voice swelled with frustration. "What the fuck."

"I know. I know."

They listened to each other breathe. She could almost feel his sigh against her cheek.

Dink cleared his throat. "I promised to be supportive, and all that, didn't I?"

Brenna smiled, even as she fought a wave of sadness. Yearning for him was mixed with a rueful triumph that his feelings were as intense as her own. "We both did. Who knew it'd be so hard, especially this soon?"

"Yeah." Small noises of activity clicked in her ear. "It's getting late. I've bothered you enough for today. Guess I'd better get moving."

"Going to work?" She flashed on the interior of the restaurant where he waited tables. Whitewashed walls and hanging light fixtures with geometric shades were softened with large leafy plants and artwork done by locals.

"Yeah, subbing for Darcy. She's going out with

Jude. Finally." The shy grad student had cast lingering glances at the darkly handsome barista in their neighborhood coffee shop for months. Community regulars had watched the halting dance of attraction between the two with great interest.

"Fantastic! I didn't think he'd ever wake up enough to notice her."

Dink snorted. "She practically ran over him a couple days ago, nearly clipped him when he crossed in front of her car. She freaked out so much he ended up trying to calm her down, 'stead of the other way around."

"Good. It's about time." But she couldn't help but envy the two.

"Yeah." Dink waited and sighed again. "Well, I gotta go."

"Okay." Brenna's hand tightened on the phone, trying to hold on to him a little longer. "Love you."

"Me, too."

The sound disappeared. Brenna slid her phone back into her pocket. If she could touch Dink, hold him for a minute and get past her sense of growing isolation, maybe the bleak mood she'd had all morning would fade. "That damned dream," she whispered, and shivered at the memory. Her hand found the projector switch and turned it on. Back to work. She cranked up her music again and began.

The next few signs weren't particularly memorable or even interesting: a hand-lettered offer of "FREE PUPPEEZ," then an ornate poster for a high school car wash. After several uninspiring samples, Brenna slumped deeper in her chair. What if most of the signs were ordinary, boring bits and pieces? What if she'd been so whacked out over Gran that she'd shot garbage? "Cut it out," she said aloud. She hadn't looked at the other reels yet. No hysteria until she'd checked out all the work.

The next reel flashed from the projector. Pictures Brenna barely recalled taking, reflections of ideas captured over two years before. It was hard to remember what common thread she'd seen among the various images. She'd been a different person then, still clinging to the idea of creating art as a contrast to the commotion she lived with, inside and out. How many times had she run out of the apartment with the heavy camera case banging against one leg, desperate to escape the small rooms that were her grandmother's prison? After Gran's move to the assisted living facility, viewing the world through her camera lens became her chief goal. Looking at life head-on was too painful. Only death was waiting for Gran, each day more strewn with the remnants of her disappearing self.

The screen filled with celestial brilliance: silver five-pointed stars floating on an indigo background in swirling, almost dizzying patterns.

"Christ on a crutch," Brenna muttered. She'd never seen this sequence before. Leaning forward in her chair, she peered more closely as the frames clicked by. It was like a take-off on Van Gogh's "Starry Night." The stars undulated on the deep blue field.

Brenna stared. Could this be something she'd stumbled across and shot without really registering it? An art installation captured at an exhibit, forgotten over time? Somebody else's piece of film somehow inserted into her reel?

What kind of bullshit is this? Had she shot that film? *Why can't I remember it?* Fear skittered along that question like a rat threading through a junkyard.

The complicated guitar solo coming through her earphones faded. What she heard instead was her grandmother's voice, hoarse and sure. "You're gonna be a star, chickie. The best director in Hollywood. You mark my words."

The stars whirled and spun in the deep blue waves.

CHAPTER 7

As Kerry wandered into the Wisdom Court kitchen, she took pleasure in the glow of the copper skillets hanging over the butcher-block island in the center of the room. Noreen was seated at the table, reading the papers in front of her.

The air was perfumed with the scent of coffee from the oversized urn bubbling on the counter. On the window sill behind it potted rosemary and sage basked in sunshine.

Rose was pulling cups out of the cupboard and setting them on a flowered tray. Strudel sat at her feet, keen brown eyes tracking her every move. Morsels had been known to drop to the floor and the dachshund would keep vigil until all food preparation was done.

"What's up?" Kerry asked. She bent to pet Strudel. "You sounded a little grim on the phone."

Rose took the lid off the owl-shaped cookie jar and began transferring its contents into a napkin-lined basket. "I need to run a couple of things by everyone, and I thought refreshments might grease the wheels."

"When don't they?" Kerry filched a cookie. "Mmm.

Chocolate chip." She propped herself against the counter and chewed with enjoyment. Her gaze was drawn back to Rose, pale in a black sweater and yoga pants. "Would this have anything to do with Max Steadman?"

Rose stepped over Strudel on her way to the refrigerator. "Wait. All will be revealed."

Kerry moved to the table and pulled out a chair.

"When the messenger appears, make him welcome, listen with a clear mind and steady heart, and remain attuned to the likelihood of danger," Noreen uttered. "Gladys Parmetter Winston, eighteen seventy-nine to nineteen thirty-three."

"Sounds a little paranoid." Kerry flicked crumbs off her denim shirt. "Disappointed by life, I suppose."

"Or by male messengers." Noreen shot her a cynical glance. "Gladys never married. Apparently no man measured up."

"Or got it up?" Kerry grinned at Noreen's pursed mouth. "Maybe she was lucky. In those days, unwedded was more likely to be bliss than hooking up with a man who believed in his divine right to rule the roost. Don't you think?"

"To be sure," countered Noreen, "so long as the woman in question had family money behind her." Impatiently she pushed her bangs off her forehead. "Remember the tyranny of economics, my dear. Without the protection of family, or of a man, few woman had the resources to keep themselves."

At a faint knock at the back door, Rose called, "Come in!"

Noreen pushed the sleeves of her crimson sweater to her elbows and fixed Kerry with a severe look. "Nowadays people smile at the endless matchmaking in Jane Austen's works, but it was no joke to the women of the time. If they didn't marry, even badly, they could go hungry."

Brenna heard the last of Noreen's words as she came through the backdoor. "Really?" She pushed back her hood but left her sweatshirt on, chilled by the breeze in the courtyard. She rubbed her hands together to warm them. "You mean starve?"

Noreen waved her into a chair. "It was a hard time for everyone, with such a gap between the lower and upper classes, and not much of a middle class at all. It was highly unusual for women to work for pay in those days, although there is the impoverished governess so beloved of fiction. Marriage was the only profession women had." She glimpsed Kerry's fleeting expression, and added, "All right, so the oldest profession *was* another."

"Coffee?" Rose asked. She set the tray of cups onto the table.

"I'd love it. That wind's getting cold." Brenna sniffed at the rich scents in the air and enjoyed the mixture of colors and textures. The room was right out of an old Selznick movie, she thought, marking the way the sunshine haloed Rose's silver-blonde curls. "I've been shivering all day."

Rose looked concerned. "Did you turn up the thermostat? I'm sure the furnaces have been lit."

"Yeah, I'm just not used to the chill." People had been wearing shorts and flip-flops when she'd left L.A.

Behind Brenna the back door opened again, letting in another gust of cold air. Andrea Bellamy came into the kitchen followed by a tall man in jeans and a thick sweater. He had amused brown eyes in a tanned, fortyish face. Andrea's cheeks were rosy and her eyes alight with happiness.

The man helped Andrea remove her denim jacket, his hands resting for a moment on her shoulders. Then his glance went beyond her to the women at the table. "Hi."

"Hey, Neal." Kerry's smirk was playful. "What've you two been up to?"

Neal raised one brow. "The pursuit of happiness."

"How constitutional of you," murmured Noreen, and Neal grinned at her wickedly.

"Neal." Andrea narrowed her eyes at him, but her lips curved in a smile. "I ran out of primer. Neal offered to take me to the art supply."

Neal nodded at Brenna. "I don't believe we've met."

Kerry followed his gaze. "Oh, sorry. This is our new associate, Brenna Payne. Brenna, meet Neal Cameron, one of the WC board members, and a tolerable guy to have around."

"Hi." Mmmm, she thought in appreciation. She'd seen more than her share of good-looking men in L.A., where being handsome was a job requirement, but this guy could give them some competition. Expressive eyes, lean build. All his own hair. She'd know a weave in a heartbeat. There were plenty of those to see in L.A. as well.

"Nice to meet you." Neal snagged a chair for Andrea, and held it for her before sitting down beside her. He glanced around the table. "So, why the powwow? And where's Aura Lee? I'm jonesing for her brownies!"

"Dentist appointment," Noreen answered. "She left a batch of chocolate chip cookies. But we ate every single one of them."

Neal's eyes closed at the blow. "A meeting with no refreshments? That sucks."

"You're too easy." Rose brought out the basket heaped with cookies and set it on the table. "You know the unspoken rule around here: no gatherings without munchies." She headed back for more provisions, shaking her head at Kerry's offer of help.

"Unspoken rule—right. You've restored my faith." He reached for a cookie. "So, the first question remains. What's going on?"

Rose brought back a carafe of coffee on another tray along with cream and a range of sweeteners. Noreen offered to serve, and began the coffee ballet of pouring and stirring.

Taking her own cup, Rose glanced around the table. "A couple of things. The first is Maxwell Steadman, the man I called you about yesterday, Neal. He's a genealogist from England here on a project commissioned by Caldicott before her death," she told the others. "The WC board has approved his working here until he's finished with it. I wanted to give you a heads-up that he'll be around for a while."

"Is he cute?" Andrea dunked a cookie into her coffee, and bore the dripping morsel to her mouth before it could drop off.

"Hey!" Neal shot her a wounded look.

She grinned as she chewed. "Artistic curiosity."

Kerry's spoon clinked against the edge of her cup as she stirred. "He's a conceited jerk," she growled. "I, for one, hope he finds what he's looking for in a hurry so he can go back where he came from."

Ouch, thought Brenna. *I wonder if the guy was trying to make a good impression?*

"*Instant enmity foretells either a mad passion or endless tiny barbs culminating in death.*"

"What?" Kerry glared at Noreen for a moment, then dissolved into giggles. "Who the *hell* came up with *that* one?"

"Me." She smiled modestly as the others laughed.

"I knew it." Kerry contemplated her with admiration. "How many others have you made up?

Come on, give."

Noreen merely stirred her coffee.

Rose watched the by-play with a smile but her eyes were shadowed with worry. "The other thing is a little more complicated." She cradled her cup in both hands. "Even strange."

"Excellent," said Noreen. "We're in need of something unusual to get us through the autumn blahs. Proceed."

"Glad to oblige. It involves my fountains—I make table fountains," Rose added for Brenna's benefit. "They're dishes filled with different stones, glass jewels, small figures—basically miniature landscapes." She moved her hands to suggest the placement of the pieces. "The rocks cover a tiny pump that sends water over the stones, producing the sound of a stream." She took a breath, let it out. "Several times lately, I've come back to nearly-finished fountains and found them taken apart, the rocks removed and set in circles around the containers."

"You'd put them together and they were taken apart again," Noreen said. It was a statement rather than a question.

Rose nodded. "As a rule I lock my workroom door and I've never found the door unlocked when I've arrived to work."

"Why do you lock it?" Neal looked at her with interest.

"It's not a question of distrust." She picked up her coffee cup and Brenna saw the tremor in her hand. "I think I need a workspace that's just mine, where I can make what I want without anybody watching me. And I need that time alone." Her smile was wry. "There's always so much going on here."

"You can say that again." Kerry reached for another cookie. "So what do you think this is about?"

Rose hesitated.

"Didn't you mention something like this before?" Noreen sent the carafe around. Andrea slid the sugar bowl and cream pitcher toward Neal.

Rose nodded. "During the summer, when Andrea was spirit-painting. One day I found a fountain container emptied, with the rocks in a circle around it."

The room was so silent they could hear a train whistle in the distance.

Brenna felt a shiver move down her back. She cleared her throat. "Sorry, but I don't know what you're talking about."

"Of course not." Rose straightened in her chair. "I guess I'd better fill you in." She recounted the events of Andrea's first week at Wisdom Court, how she'd begun to sketch and paint, while in a trance, images of a man she'd never before seen.

Brenna automatically watched the others as she listened to Rose. Though they obviously knew the story, their reactions were mixed. Andrea captured Neal's hand in her own, and he clasped her fingers, slanting her an odd smile.

Kerry's cheeks reddened as Rose explained her skepticism about the possible causes of Andrea's dilemma. Only Noreen appeared detached, almost insulated from the emotions experienced by the others. *She's the analytical one,* thought Brenna, more used to observing than participating in situations. But how could she have seen what Rose was talking about and not have a strong emotional reaction?

Rose's air of discomfort grew as she described their efforts to determine the source of Andrea's apparent connection with people who had lived in the Wisdom Court house generations before. She ended with their failed séance.

"Besides everything else, Aura Lee was convinced that Caldicott was trying to send her messages," Rose added. "Not that she could ever decipher anything, but she still believes those communications are being sent."

Brenna was aware of a deep excitement. What an amazing movie the story would make. It had everything—a mystery, star-crossed lovers, revenge, a séance, and great possibilities for action scenes.

"It was a very difficult time," Noreen was saying. "Though undeniably interesting."

Brenna took a deep breath, knowing she had to chill. She could hardly start raving about making a film based on what she'd just heard. "So, if I understand what you're saying, you believe you were dealing with a haunting?"

Kerry groaned. "Jeez, I hate that word! It makes my skin crawl every time I hear it."

"What would you prefer?" Noreen asked pointedly. "Visitation? Ghostly gathering? Spirit convention? Remember, you saw a couple of strange things yourself."

"Not that I don't sympathize with how you feel," Neal said to Kerry, "but you were here. You remember what it was like."

"I remember." Kerry waved a hand toward Andrea. "I still wish you'd cop to temporary insanity. Then I wouldn't have to be so damned open-minded about it."

"You? Open-minded?" Noreen's voice was dust-dry.

"Sticks and stones," Kerry shot back.

"Enough!" Rose looked as surprised as the others at her outburst. She turned toward Brenna. "Yes, we tend to think of it as a haunting. And it stopped when we figured it out. But now this business with the fountains has me spooked." She glanced around the table, clearly troubled. "What if it's starting up again?"

Andrea shook her head. "Rose, don't even think about such a thing." Neal put his arm around her shoulders and pulled her close, but it didn't appear to help. "I don't think I could stand to go through it again," she whispered.

The back door flew open and slammed against the wall. Cold air filled the kitchen.

"Jesus!" Kerry jumped to her feet and ran to close it.

"We probably didn't shut it all the way," Neal murmured, tightening his hold on Andrea.

"Right," she said. Her face was ashen.

Brenna watched, wanting to ask her about her experience, wondering if she'd actually *felt* the presence of another entity. But now was not the time. Andrea looked ready to run out of the room. That, or faint dead away.

"If we learned anything from what you went through, Andrea," said Rose, "it's that we have to talk to each other about this stuff." She looked around the table. "We couldn't help Andrea till we started comparing notes. That's why I'm telling you now about the fountains. If someone—something—is here trying to communicate with us, we have to face it together."

CHAPTER 8

Red organza drapes smothered the light at the windows, giving a cavernous feel to the bedroom. Candles on the dresser and headboard, on the nightstand and bookshelf, provided the only illumination. The reflected flames danced in the oval mirror above the bureau, burnishing the gilded frame.

Aura Lee sat at a writing table encircled by a line of sea salt on the carpeted floor. She wore a dull gold robe, and her brassy curls were held in an upsweep by two onyx combs. Gold shadow had been applied to her eyelids, and every one of her fingers bore a ring. In front of her, along the rear edge of the desk, were three pottery dishes, each heaped with a different herb. At the end of this row was an empty crystal wineglass. As she struck a match, holding it successively to each of the dishes, she whispered,

> *"Spirits who have passed beyond,*
>
> *I call to one of whom I'm fond.*
>
> *I ask for guidance, pray for aid,*
>
> *To understand the signals made.*

For clarity, for meaning true,

Presence, I now ask: ensue."

The pungent smoke from the three dishes of dittany, balm of Gilead, and amaranth wafted upward, drifting into the currents created by the candles. Aura Lee breathed deeply, eyes closed, sitting motionless for a long moment. She tugged open the center drawer of the desk and peered into it. From it she pulled a thick paper with uneven edges upon which were written the letters of the English alphabet in three rows. At the top of the page, the word HELLO was in the left corner, the word GOODBYE in the right. On the bottom of the page, the word YES was in the right corner, the word NO in the left. She upended the crystal wineglass and placed it on the paper.

Aura Lee closed her eyes again and chanted softly,

"Goblet placed to spell your meaning,

Parchment ready to reveal.

Part the veil intervening,

Let your signal break the seal."

Resting her fingertips on the edge of the base, she again closed her eyes. "Come to me, Cottie. Please." Her whisper was faint, but heartfelt.

Her eyes flew open at the tiny tremble of the glass. Aura Lee held her breath as it moved, shivering into life, then slid slowly across the paper toward HELLO. When the glass stopped atop the word, she sagged in her chair. "Cottie? Is that you?"

Under her fingertips the wineglass began to move, this time toward the bottom of the page, coming to rest over the word YES.

Her breathing uneven, Aura Lee bent toward the glass, trying to get closer to it or to what moved it. "Oh, Cottie. I knew it, I knew if I kept trying…" Her fingers shook on the edge of the stem base and the wineglass rattled against the paper and the desk beneath it. "No," she muttered fearfully, "mustn't tip it." She inhaled again, struggling to contain her feelings.

The glass was motionless. Aura Lee waited, taking shallow breaths. Then it stirred, swerving toward a letter on the paper. "M," she whispered.

The glass moved on to the letter I. In a slow, faltering dance, it slid next to R, moved off it and then returned again to the R. "M-I-R-R…" whispered Aura Lee. The glass glided to the O and back again to the R. There it stopped.

"M-I-R-R-O-R." Aura Lee studied the letters on the paper, her fingers still resting on the stem base. "Mirror?" she asked in a puzzled voice. "Is that what you mean, Cottie? Mirror?"

The wineglass twitched and slid toward the YES at the bottom of the paper.

Aura Lee was still, waiting for the wineglass to move again, but it remained stationary. Finally she lifted her gaze to search the room. "Cottie, I don't understand what you mean." Immediately, the glass began to vibrate, and soon afterward moved, more quickly this time, among the letters: M-I-R-R-O-R.

Aura Lee's lips trembled with her effort to hold back the flood of words she longed to speak. "I don't know what you mean. What about a mirror, Cottie?" Her voice quavered on the name.

The wineglass beneath her fingers was still. In the silent room the aroma of burning herbs intensified. From the corners of her eyes, Aura Lee glanced at the deepening shadows, unconscious of the shudder moving through her.

In an instant the candle flames went out. Aura Lee gasped, her attention drawn to the mirror above the bureau. Within the oval frame the murky reflection of the room roiled with swirling clouds. From the center of the vortex, a glowing light sparked and grew, resolving into the features of a woman's face. Her eyes were large and imploring, her cheeks ashen, her countenance intent.

Aura Lee strove to breathe, horror spreading through her as the image in the mirror sharpened into clarity. The woman stared at her, and in a jerky, horrifying effort moved her mouth, struggling to speak. Aura Lee let out a shriek and pushed away from the desk. The crystal wineglass rolled off the edge and shattered on the floor.

"Rose? Rose!" Aura Lee hammered on the workroom door. "I know you're there. Let me in. Let me in now!" She waited as Rose unlocked the door. It swung open. "Hurry! It's important."

Moments ago Rose had felt the day would never end. She was tired of Wisdom Court, of the problems, of questions with no answers. If she hid for a while, perhaps she could come to terms with what was wearing away at her. Now she saw Aura Lee, heard the tremor in her voice, noted signs of tears. And wished she could be alone. "What is it?"

Aura Lee pushed past her and collapsed into the fat chair with the worn blue corduroy cover. She didn't wait for Rose to sit down opposite her. "I made contact today." She was rubbing her hands together as if they were cold, though the room was still warm from the afternoon sun. "I used some amaranth with the dittany and balm of Gilead, and—"

"Skip that part," Rose said. "What's going on?"

"Yes, I'll tell you." Aura Lee's voice trembled. "I was trying to reach Cottie, and I did it. Oh, God, Rose. I did it. She spoke to me—well, she didn't speak, exactly, but she did show herself."

Rose sighed inwardly, wanting to put her head in her hands. Was this for real? Trying to tiptoe through the minefields of Aura Lee's obsession wasn't easy on an ordinary day, let alone now. "What do you mean?"

Aura Lee swallowed and dabbed at her forehead with a handkerchief. Her hands were shaking. Rose looked more closely at her pale cheeks and the bewilderment in her eyes. "I used a makeshift Ouija board. I know, I know," she added before Rose could respond. "It's an amateurish trick, but I thought it might work. And it *did*." She began rubbing her hands together again. She laughed a short, shocked chuckle, sending a cold shiver down Rose's spine. "It did work."

Rose realized something had terrified her. "What happened?"

Aura Lee glanced up from her hands. "I was going to ask for clarification. You know, to explain what's going on with your fountain rocks. But I asked for Cottie to come and she did. And what she spelled out on the Ouija was strange. I didn't understand it," she babbled. "It spelled out *MIRROR.* Twice it spelled out *MIRROR.*"

"That's it?" Rose tried to figure out why the word would be so shattering, but nothing occurred to her. "Why is that so upsetting?"

"That's not what upset me—" Aura Lee stopped and then burst out with, "I saw her face in *my* mirror." Aura Lee's features twisted, and it took her a moment's struggle to go on. "I saw her, Rose. I saw her."

"Who?"

"*Who*? Cottie! I saw her face in my mirror! She appeared there!" Aura Lee stared into Rose's eyes with desperation.

Oh, Lord, Rose thought. What do I say? What *can* I say?

"Didn't you hear me?" Aura Lee demanded. "I'm not joking. It happened. I really did see her."

"In your mirror."

"*Yes*." Aura Lee laced her fingers together, but they pulled apart and she wrung her hands.

"What was she doing?" Rose asked in spite of herself.

"She looked so troubled. I always thought if I did reach her, she would be happy. But she didn't look happy at all." It was a cry of distress, and Aura Lee pressed her lips together to silence herself.

"She stared at me, and I acted like a ninny. I was scared——scared of Cottie! I probably hurt her feelings, gaping at her like a fool. But it shocked me, seeing her like that." Tears were slipping down Aura Lee's cheeks. Her words tumbled over each other more quickly as she tried to explain herself.

Rose pushed herself out of her chair and came around the worktable. "It's all right," she said as she put her arm around Aura Lee. "Hush now, it's all right."

Aura Lee leaned into her for a moment and wept. Then she straightened. "No. It's not all right. It's anything *but* all right. If you could've seen the expression on her face—so haggard, so troubled. And all I could do was sit there." She looked up at Rose, radiating distress. "We have to do something to help her. This isn't just a parlor game anymore, Rose. Cottie needs our help and we've got to give it."

Rose felt at such a loss. Where to begin to unravel this unholy mess? "She's dead, Aura Lee. How can we change that or any of the circumstances surrounding the fact?" She patted Aura Lee's arm, wanting to soothe her desperation. "I can't imagine anything for us to do. I haven't got a clue."

"I can't help but feel I let her down." Aura Lee dabbed at her eyes with a tissue pulled from her pocket. "I've been babbling on about connecting with the Other Side, and when it happens, I fall apart. I'm ashamed of myself. I didn't help Cottie at all."

Rose tried to shake off a growing sense of unreality. "Just listen to yourself. You're talking about an—an *extraordinary* event. How many people could handle seeing a ghost in the mirror?" *How many would believe it if they did*, she added to herself. *And what the hell am I going to do about this? Did Aura Lee really see Caldicott Wyntham? Had she been right all along in her belief that Cottie was trying to get through to them?*

Aura Lee looked up at Rose, her features hardening. "I thought I was ready to see apparitions, and everything that comes with them. I'm supposed to be a professional, Rose. A seeker of truth in however many worlds there are! I didn't just let Cottie down today. I let myself down." She crumpled the tissue in her hand and pushed herself out of the chair. "I won't let my failure be the final word in this matter. I'll contact Cottie again. And next time I won't get woozy and act like an idiot. Next time I'll find out what's wrong with her. She needs our help, Rose, and I'm going to see that she gets it." Aura Lee marched to the door and, with a grand gesture, flung it open and swept through it.

Rose closed her mouth and sank into the old chair.

CHAPTER 9

Brenna shoveled the last of the sesame tofu into her mouth and closed the carton as she chewed. The Imperial Lotus wasn't bad, she thought. Decent food, reasonably cheap, speedy delivery. And it didn't clash with the Australian Shiraz. Who could ask for more?

The fortune cookie wrapper crackled in the silent kitchen. Even the refrigerator had stopped running. "I need some music," Brenna said aloud and wished she hadn't.

She shot a look at the window over the sink. The panes were darkening—time to go back to the studio. The feeling that someone she couldn't see was looking in at her was freaking her out. Way too Freddie Kruger. *Gotta stop forgetting to ask Rose for some damned curtains.*

She hunched her shoulders. Sliding the fortune cookie out of its sleeve, she broke it in half. "Your lover will arrive tonight," she chanted hopefully before looking at it. If only.

The small strip of paper unfolded between her fingers. She peered at the tiny print, frowning. She could make out: *Kind acts result in new friends*, or so she thought. Over the printed words someone had clumsily scratched another message in what looked like gray ink. *Behind circle.*

"Weird," Brenna muttered. *So much for quality control at the old fortune cookie factory.* She crumpled the paper and tossed it, aiming for the sink, but it fell short. "Balls." She pushed herself out of the chair to retrieve it and threw it in the wastebasket.

Her eyes were bleary after screening film all afternoon. Most of the canisters she'd brought from California had been developed. A few hadn't surfaced since she hadn't unpacked everything yet. Raymond, the deliveryman, had brought another batch of film the day before and she'd been reviewing a series of coastal shots. Back when she'd shot the footage she'd played with the idea of creatures from an ancient race of beings still hiding in the craggy formations carved by wind and waves. To counter the evil sorcery at work in her grandmother's brain she'd sought evidence of magic, of a secret language of affirmation in the world around her. "I was wicked crazy then," she whispered. Maybe she still was.

Brenna rubbed her eyes and raised her arms toward the ceiling, reaching with her fingers toward the white shell patterns in the plaster. She had in her mind an image of Dink stretching out his back muscles after hours spent hunched over his guitar. He'd always made her think of a tawny cat luxuriating in his flexibility.

A mixture of longing and desolation rose in her. "Okay, okay, back to work."

The studio was dim, and she realized why the uncovered overhead windows here didn't bother her like the ones in the kitchen. *Because I can't be seen.*

Brenna loaded the next reel onto the projector and made herself comfortable in the plush chair next to it.

She hummed music from the 20th Century Fox opening logo and pushed the ON button.

"Oh, God, more waves." Here were similar shots of tidal waters swirling at the base of a large haystack rock chiseled by the wind. What was it she'd been after that day? The suggestion of a gargoyle face threatening to emerge from the rough stone?

Before her eyes, the rock vanished from the shot, leaving only the water on the screen. The waves began to rotate, almost in a whirlpool, and as she watched, stars replaced the water, five-pointed stars swirling round and round. "Holy shit," she whispered. The glowing stars spilled onto the shoreline and then slid back, some remaining behind, caught on the sand.

Barely breathing, Brenna stared at the screen as the film went through the sprockets. The end of the reel slapped against the body of the projector until she reached over to turn it off. Stars, like the stars from the first reel she'd viewed several days before, had been added to her shot. But how could someone add those onto film? Okay, there were ways: animation, computer-generated images and the like. But why would somebody do that to her film? And *who*?

She turned on the lights and stared at the silent projector. Well, she could rule out the idea of her memory playing tricks on her. This was something else, somebody trying to mess with her. *I guess I'll just have to mess with them.* But where could she start looking for answers? The developing people, for a start, but that would have to wait until tomorrow.

Dink. She relaxed a little at the thought of him. He could listen, maybe even have some ideas about what was happening.

Brenna reached into her pocket for her cell phone even as she realized it wasn't there. A quick glance at the chair—nothing. Where was the last place? She'd left it in the kitchen when she ordered the Chinese. She walked from the studio through the short hallway, spying the cell on the table as she came through the door.

As she scooped up the phone, Brenna saw the small folded piece of paper on the table. She reached for it and flashed on the fortune cookie. Her hand froze. The sequence of events clicked in her mind: unfolding the fortune and reading it. Missing the sink when she tossed it. Then she'd picked it up off the floor and thrown it away. *Is somebody else in the house*? She spun around to look behind her. Heart in her throat, she lunged for the door to check the bolt. It was locked.

Nobody was going to leap out of a closet. Brenna headed back to the kitchen, her footsteps slowing as she got to the door and saw the dark windows beyond. *God, I'm pathetic.* Between tripping out over nightmares and freaking at bare windows, she was turning her chance at the big time into a Hitchcock movie. And not one of the Cary Grant films.

She went back to the table and looked at the paper. She took a breath and unfolded the narrow strip, her pulse pounding in her ears. *Kind acts result in new friends*, she read. The words *behind circle* were gone.

"I don't get what you're talking about." The man behind the counter at Images and Dreams hadn't paid much attention as Brenna described the stars on her film. "We developed what you gave us and Raymond delivered it. That's it."

His face was tight with irritation and Brenna couldn't find a hint of customer service in his small, close-set eyes. She pulled the reel from her satchel. "No, that's not it. Two reels I've had now with stars on the film that I didn't put there. Either your equipment is screwed up or somebody working here is adding stuff for some screwed up reason."

"Let me see that." He snatched at the reel and headed toward the door behind him.

Brenna hurried to the end of the counter. "I'm coming with you." No way was she going to let this asshole do anything with her film unless she watched him do it.

He growled something as she followed him into the tech room. When he pulled a chair over to a desk that held a 16mm film splicer, she said, "Hey, wait a minute," but he overrode her.

"I have to check it." He decanted the film and pushed the reel onto the sprocket and laid the celluloid across the steel film tracks, then threaded the end onto the empty reel.

Brenna had relaxed a bit when she saw the Craig kit he was using. He was abrupt, but his hands moved with care as he cued up the film and switched on the viewing light. He began to advance the film with the rewind handle.

She watched the images move on the small viewing screen, shoulders tightening as the end of the film drew near. There, she thought, there's the rock, the waves swirling around it, so now the rock would disappear, the whirlpool of stars would start circling...The rock remained, the waves surging around it, and the waves lapped against the shore. The segment ended.

"So, what stars?" he snarled.

Her gaze jerked from the screen to his face and his sour smirk slid into a cynical frown. "What's going on? You on drugs or something?"

"No." She reached over his shoulder to pull the reel off the machine and fumbled to put it into the can. "Sorry I bothered you."

"Here, let me do that." He slid the cover onto the can and handed it to her.

"Thanks." Brenna gripped the canister and headed out of the room, the man following behind.

"You okay?"

"Sure. Thanks for checking the film. Sorry about the mix-up."

When the door closed behind her, Brenna felt the steel in her spine starting to melt. She hurried to the car Rose lent her and unlocked it. By the time she fastened her seatbelt she'd encased the fear in ice. She'd had lots of practice at that, her go-to reaction until she was alone.

Jesus, what if it's in you?

She shoved the panicky question out of her mind and drove back to Wisdom Court.

NIGHTMIRROR

The narrow passage goes one way, past shadows along baseboards, past tacked-on smiles and hollow words.

She steps on marching squares until she faces the door. *Step on a crack and break your mother's back.* Already broken.

A nightmare door with fear behind holds paper shapes to hide what's true.

Photos taped inside the room are frozen moments flat as skipping stones no longer thrown at memories.

Mirror, mirror on the wall looks past the stranger there, reflects the stranger come to watch.

Soft afghan on the bed, has colors worn, and stitches loose. The yarn unravels every time, patterns fading, twisted strands left lying.

The smiling faces praise: all will be well. They move in careful patterns, no upset here, no wild grief, no surging hate at ruin.

But wolves should howl at the waning moon and claws should slash the way things are.

CHAPTER 10

Kerry turned away from the south library window and buttoned the green cardigan she'd added to her jeans and white shirt. She glanced at Max Steadman. He'd settled at the oak table upon his arrival an hour before. Stacked in front of him were Caldicott Wyntham's journals. Max was a skimmer, quickly sorting through the first few volumes. Not that there was much in any of them to linger over.

Max turned a page, and the slight noise brought her gaze back to him. In the three days since he'd last been at Wisdom Court, she'd convinced herself her prickly reaction to him had been the result of work frustration, nothing to do with sexual interest. Today the anemic light through the windowpanes displayed all too clearly his lean body in corduroy slacks and navy sweater over a white oxford shirt. The bronze ceiling lamp above the table shone on his hair, highlighting a few strands of silver, as well as his thick lashes.

Kerry focused on the gray hairs rather than the eyelashes. Such signs of mortality were reassuring because what she'd discovered about him from her on-line search had made him appear all too rarified for her tastes. He'd taken a first at Balliol in history, his thesis on the seeds of modern time concepts found in medieval social orders published by Oxford University Press.

She'd greeted him, and shown him to the pile of books. He'd ignored her since. Her saner self felt like a nitpicking manager-trainee. So what if he spent the rest of the day here? She wasn't responsible for his activities.

"Are you going to hover over me while I'm here?" His clipped accent cut through her muddled thoughts.

"I'm not hovering." Kerry could feel the color rising in her cheeks, but soldiered on. "I was thinking about my work, if you must know."

Max shot her a look. "Ah, yes. Your biography of Caldicott Wyntham." Deliberately he shut the journal in front of him. "I hope it has more to offer than the lists of activities necessary in building Wisdom Court. Along with the ongoing cast of characters involved in the process, that's all I've discovered in these volumes."

Kerry shrugged. She hated feeling defensive. "You can't fault Caldicott for keeping on top of details." Carefully she seated herself at the end of the table. "Good institutional history is important, too."

Max leaned back in his chair, one brow arched in disbelief. "It's like reading stock reports: stultifying unless you have money riding on the outcomes. Don't tell me you find them of interest."

She was going to lie, but her gaze collided with the challenge in his blue eyes. "No." Kerry pushed one hand through her hair in annoyance. "My heart doesn't race at accounting figures and meeting minutes. I've had to read them, though, just to cover the bases. And the associates' information over the years is interesting. There've been some outstanding ones."

"Certainly, but I'm looking for more family history." Max glanced around the rectangular room at the shelves of books lining the walls. "Some anecdotes about her life would be helpful. What else is here?"

"Basic stuff, but all of it strictly Wisdom Court era. Nothing older than fifty years ago." Kerry sighed, unaware of how discouraged she sounded. "I've checked over everything I've been able to find."

Max was silent for a long moment. "You talked to her before she died?" he asked finally.

"Yes. She told me she had the information I was asking for: diaries, documents, all of it. She said she would turn over everything." Kerry trailed off. The taste of failure rose in her like bile.

"She died before you saw any of it," Max murmured.

Kerry nodded. "I don't think she meant to mess things up, but she ran out of time."

He didn't say anything. Kerry steeled herself to meet disdain in his expression, but when she actually looked at him he was staring out the window. She waited, and finally he turned back to her. "Why do you think she put off giving you what you needed to write the book?"

"No clue." Kerry pushed herself away from the table, out of the chair. "If I did know, I'd be further along than I am now." He didn't respond, and in the heavy silence she realized she was waiting for him to criticize her for lack of foresight, for not pinning down Caldicott, for not having finished the biography. I don't need *him* to do that, she thought impatiently. I've done enough of it myself.

"You realize, of course, that it's a treasure hunt." He

stood up slowly, favoring his left leg. His smile was sympathetic. "We could view it as an opportunity to work together. An adventure."

Kerry snorted. Presumably he was after the same information she needed, but what would he do with it? "You're suggesting we tiptoe through the attics together? Why?"

"Why not?" He looked at her thoughtfully. "Think of it as a way for us both to achieve a tactical advantage. We join forces, and whatever we find, we share."

Kerry shook her head. "You won't be here long enough to share anything. You'll be off on your next escapade, digging up some other person's family skeletons."

"You're missing my point." His tone was polite, but his narrowed eyes were cooling with irritation. "I'm not going anywhere until I've completed the job I agreed to do for Ms. Wyntham. As it happens, I liked her a great deal and I feel I owe it to her to fulfill our contract. Until I—or *we*—find this supposed trove of information, I'm remaining here. And my work is not a series of *escapades*." He bit off the words with precision.

"Got it." Kerry nodded stiffly and headed out of the library.

"Where are you going?" he demanded from behind her, but she didn't answer. Her shoulder knocked against the front door lintel as she passed through it but she didn't feel anything. Her bad temper was rapidly escalating into rage, and not knowing exactly why made her even angrier. The cold air stung her face as she strode toward the east associate house, and she realized she'd left her jacket in the library. I'll get it later, she thought, after he's gone back to the hotel.

She'd just unlocked the outer door when her arm

was grabbed and she was pulled round. Max tightened his hold and tugged her inside to her flat door. He dragged it open and pushed her through it into the foyer. "What the devil is the matter with you?" he demanded. "I can't decide if you're rude or simply demented. You're acting as if I've offended you. I offered to work with you," he shouted. "Full partners."

Kerry had thought him bloodless. She was wrong. Max was furious, eyes blazing blue fire. His hands were clenched at his sides, no doubt restraining himself from wringing her neck. When the corner of his mouth twisted in aggravation she was swept with the desire to lift her mouth to his, to kiss him for all she was worth. A single step would bring her close enough to reach him. She started toward him, but awareness of what she was doing hit her like a splash of cold water.

What would he think of me? She stepped back, hitting the wall behind her.

Max's brows twitched together in a frown. "I didn't mean to frighten you," he muttered. "I've got a bloody awful temper and you manage to incite it more often than not."

"I'm not frightened." Kerry let out a breath. Her lips were throbbing, and a part of her wanted to walk right into his arms. She stole a glance at him.

Max scowled at her. "I don't ordinarily behave in such a fashion."

Kerry fought embarrassment. "I was rude to you first. I've been so upset over not finding Caldicott's papers, and it felt like you were judging, and...let *me* do the honors. I apologize." She extended her hand, which he took automatically.

"What do you mean, about my judging?"

Kerry shrugged. "I was probably projecting my own

feelings onto you." She slipped her hand out of his. "I don't have much more time here at Wisdom Court, so I'm getting more than a little frantic."

"I meant what I said about our pooling resources."

"I appreciate the offer. Can you stay now and talk about how we might work together?" At his nod, Kerry led him into the living room and turned on the light. "Please sit down."

Max surveyed the papers strewn across the overstuffed sofa cushions, his gaze rebounding off the chair draped with several sweaters and a coat. "Where?"

"Oh, for God's sake," Kerry gathered the papers and jackets and tossed everything behind the sofa. "The temperature keeps changing. I never know what coat to wear. Here, sit." Heading for the kitchen, she called over her shoulder, "What can I get you to drink?"

"I hate to live up to the cliché," he said mildly as he seated himself, "but do you have any tea?"

"Sure." Kerry headed for the stove. Every nerve in her body was thrumming. She paused long enough to wonder what might have happened if she'd kissed him. Squaring her shoulders, she filled the kettle and turned on the burner.

What did she have to go with tea? Cookies, there'd been some she'd begged from Aura Lee. After a quick scramble, she found them in the refrigerator. Six left, she thought proudly. Maybe she was finally tapping into her hidden self-control.

"Have you gone out the back way?" The dryness in the inquiry carried well from the living room.

"I'm putting the kettle on," she called back. "You can come out here if you want."

A few moments later he appeared in the doorway, open book in hand. "Where did you find this?" He held out the copy of his own book, *The Vocabulary of*

Time: Medieval Thought and Modern Idiom.

Kerry hadn't meant to let him know she'd been checking him out. "I saw the title in your CV and thought it sounded interesting."

"Of course you did." He set the book onto the countertop and patiently cleared a stack of books off one of the oak chairs at the square table. He sat down and proceeded to examine the volumes piled on the other side.

"I've been cross-referencing citations about Wisdom Court, as well as Caldicott wherever I can find them," Kerry explained. She frowned at how many books she'd left lying around. And of course she'd left a note for the cleaning service to leave them where they lay.

"Mmmph." Max was reading from a leather-bound edition.

She didn't ask him what kind of tea he wanted. It was moot, since all she had were several herbal teas and three bags in the bottom of a box of Earl Grey. The scent of bergamot drifted from the flowered teapot as she poured the hot water. The six precious chocolate chip cookies were on a plate. Napkins, spoons, sugar. No cream, just milk.

Kerry glanced toward the table to see Max leafing through yet another of the books. He appeared perfectly relaxed, no uncomfortable musing going on in *his* mind. He was here for afternoon tea. She gathered everything onto a tray and took it to the table. Max looked up at her with a smile. She felt a flutter somewhere in the region of her chest.

She parceled out supplies. "I've been thinking. About working together, I mean. It might be feasible."

Max nodded, the gleam back in his eyes.

"Here, let me pour the tea," Kerry said hastily. As she lifted the flowered teapot, the book Max had set on the countertop fell to the floor. Kerry's hand jerked and tea splashed onto the table. "Oops, I'll get a paper towel."

Max got up to retrieve the book from the floor. As he lifted it, a paper fluttered from between the pages, landing near his feet. He bent again to pick up the scrap, glancing at it as he returned to the table.

Kerry wiped up the spilled tea and threw away the paper towel. "Let's try this again." She filled the cups and set one in front of Max. "Milk?" When he didn't answer, she looked inquiringly at him. His face was expressionless, his mouth a straight line. "Something wrong?"

Max held the paper out to her. When she read the handwritten words on it, Kerry felt the air rush out of her lungs. *Personal Journal: 1939-1945.* The page was torn on one edge, and she could see the holes where it had been bound into a volume.

Kerry's mind whirled as she studied the page. She knew the handwriting as well as she knew her own. "Where did this come from?"

"Spare me the amateur theatrics." Max's voice was cold. "That's written in the hand of Caldicott Wyntham. I've been reading insipid journal entries in that same writing throughout the morning." He closed the pages of his book and carefully placed it on the table. "I sympathized with your predicament. I was sincere about our working together to find more information. Amusing, isn't it?" He stood up and pushed his chair snug against the table. "If you didn't want to share information about her, then you should simply have told me."

Kerry's eyes widened. He thought she was lying? She glanced back down at the paper, and the sight of the familiar pen strokes made her head swim.

Max walked out of the room and toward the front

door. Kerry jumped to her feet and hurried after him. "Max, please don't go. I don't know where it came from."

Max paused at the door. "What nonsense. I can't fathom what game you're at, but I don't appreciate being played for a fool." He grasped the doorknob and turned it.

Kerry put her hand over his to stop him. "Max, please listen to me. I swear I've never seen that paper before. I honestly don't know where it came from." Darkness lined the edges of her vision, and she was beginning to feel peculiar.

Max studied her, his face harsh with disbelief. As he read her eyes, his own widened. "I think you believe what you say." He released the doorknob. "Then tell me this: if you have no other source of Ms. Wyntham's journals, where could that excerpt have possibly originated? It was in that copy of my book. Where was it before today?"

Kerry noted from a distance that her knees felt rubbery. It occurred to her that standing was becoming a precarious proposition. She walked clumsily toward the sofa, but didn't quite make it that far. Without warning her legs gave out and she sat down hard on the floor.

CHAPTER 11

The hot afternoon air held its breath. Even the sparrows nesting in the ivy creeping up the walls of the house were silent.

Aura Lee sat in the bentwood rocking chair in her bedroom. In the soft light of the table lamp, she peered at the dog-eared pages of a book on herbs. The leather cover was frayed along the edges and bore dark stains. Her friend Ruth Ann had made her promise to return the herbal in three day's time, swearing that her keeping it any longer would corrupt the power of the book. Aura Lee didn't believe that, but the feeling she got from holding the book made her anxious to return it.

Aura Lee turned another page, wondering how she could get in closer contact with Cottie's spirit. Would a recipe or charm help? Plants had been used from ancient times to increase the powers of those who followed the old ways. Echinacea could strengthen spells, according to one source she'd read. Another taught that lavender leaves would heighten her ability to see Cottie when she revealed herself. Aura Lee had already tucked the herb into her pockets.

The entry for rosemary in *Cunningham's Encyclopedia of Magical Herbs* was initially promising: *If you wish to receive knowledge or the answer to a question, burn rosemary on charcoal and smell its smoke.* But the next bit bothered her: *Rosemary is also grown to attract elves...* Enough was going on without adding elves to the situation.

She was afraid to use the Ouija board again. Aura Lee shivered at the memory of Caldicott's face taking shape in the mirror. She darted a glance at the oval glass over the bureau and returned her gaze to the open book. If she hadn't been so frightened the last time, Cottie might have spoken to her. The thought still galled her. Her own fear had prevented a complete connection. She wouldn't even try again until she knew how to control it.

Aura Lee's eyes narrowed as she came to a paragraph in the herbal about the thistle plant. *Thistle can be a medium for communion with the spirits that have passed beyond the mortal coil. After thrice blessing the pot, place sprigs in water brought to a boil. When the steam floats above the vessel, call to those spirits you seek. Await their utterances.* "Of course," she murmured. "Thistle." It could be like a phone call, with the steam conveying both her words as well as the response from Cottie. Aura Lee stifled a smile at the thought. Humor didn't mix with raising the dead.

The scent of cinnamon drifted through the room. Before Aura Lee could identify its source, a shaft of light sneaked through a space between the organza drapes, finding some of the crystals hanging near the window, scattering off into rainbow glitters. She went to the window to block out the sun, but when she reached the curtains she heard a soft humming. As she turned back toward the bureau, she saw a flash from the silver tray holding several cut-glass perfume bottles. The polished surface began to glow, and the vials refracted the light. The humming deepened.

In dread Aura Lee approached the dresser. Pools of light were moving like living things trapped inside the metal. The hum grew to a higher, louder pitch. Aura Lee cupped her hands over her ears to muffle the sound.

The palm of a hand pressed up against the surface of the silver and Aura Lee fell back with a cry. The silver parted like water and transparent fingers reached to grasp at the bottles.

Aura Lee staggered to the door. The tone intensified, now a whine throbbing through the room.

"By the Goddess!" Aura Lee clutched the doorknob, nearly wrenching it from the wood. But the knob didn't turn, and as the volume built even more, she hammered on the door with both hands. "Let me out! Help me! Get me out!"

The door was thrust open from the other side, throwing Aura Lee off balance. Rose and Noreen ran to her and grabbed her arms, pulling her from the room. As they spilled into the hallway, Noreen spun to yank the door shut. Behind it abrupt silence fell.

Aura Lee sobbed as she stumbled toward the parlor sofa and collapsed onto it. Ashen-faced, Noreen lowered herself into the striped chair and looked back at the door with shocked eyes. "What in heaven's name *was* that?"

Rose ran into the nearby bathroom and swung the door closed behind her. Choking, gagging sounds soon followed.

When Rose rejoined them, Noreen had moved to the couch to sit beside Aura Lee, and was patting her shoulder. Noreen was still deeply shaken, but her eyes were alive with excitement. She noted Rose's pallor.

"Are you all right?"

"Oh, sure." Rose wended her way through the clutter of furniture, catching her long gray sweatshirt on the curlicue of an art deco lamp. Finally she sank into the gold damask chair opposite the sofa. She looked at Aura Lee. "Are you in any shape to talk?"

Aura Lee had stopped crying, but she was trembling helplessly. Brass-colored hair tumbled around her pasty face. "Yes," she whispered. "Yes."

"What happened in there?" Rose glanced over her shoulder at Aura Lee's bedroom. "It sounded like the hounds of hell."

Aura Lee gulped and quavered, "Don't say that."

Noreen was shivering, rubbing her arms to warm them. "I've never heard anything like it. You must have conjured up something incredible this time."

"I didn't do anything." Aura Lee's voice shook. "I was reading a book, that's all." At the disbelief in Noreen's gaze she blurted, "I was doing research. That's all." She sobbed once, and covered her mouth with both hands.

"No chants?" Noreen asked brusquely, but her eyes were kind. "No appeals to the Great Beyond?" She shuddered again in spite of herself.

Rose stood up and headed for the door to the main kitchen. Within moments she was back with a bottle in one hand and three teacups rattling from the fingers of the other. Lining up the cups on the coffee table, she poured brandy into them and handed them to Noreen and Aura Lee. "Slam it," she directed and carried out her own instructions. Eyes watering, she coughed sharply, but her shoulders relaxed.

Aura Lee sipped, made a face, and gulped the rest.

Noreen's wrist-flick and brisk swallow were efficient. She caught Rose's half-smile and said, "I *was* headmistress at a girls' school."

Rose sank back into her chair. "Some days I think mainlining the stuff is the only way I'll survive this job."

The three women sat quietly, each lost in her own thoughts. Finally Rose straightened in the chair. "I have absolutely no idea what happened here. I know you're upset, Aura Lee, but you have to tell us what you were doing."

Aura Lee explained how she'd been searching for ways to strengthen the connection with Caldicott. "I didn't try any charms or spells," she declared. "I was too afraid to."

Rose lifted a hand. "I believe you. Tell me what happened next."

Aura Lee's brow puckered. "It began when I went to the window to adjust the drapes."

"Why did you do that?" Noreen interjected.

Aura Lee blinked. "Because sunlight was coming through and I wanted to darken the room. That's when the humming began. I turned to look for what was causing that and I saw the tray beginning to glow."

Noreen's eyes widened. "That would be the—"

"The tray where I have my perfume bottles." Aura Lee's hand shook as she brought it to her forehead. "Cottie gave it to me on my silver anniversary at Wisdom Court. She wrapped it in Irish linen." Her lips trembled and her voice died.

"You showed it to me," Rose said gently. "It's quite lovely."

Aura Lee nodded. "I went over to the tray to see what the light was. I thought maybe the sun had hit it just right." She shook her head. "It wasn't the sun. Light was moving around *inside* it. And the humming was getting louder. It was when the hand moved inside the tray that I got scared. The humming was so loud it hurt my ears, and fingers broke through the surface…I tried to get out but the door wouldn't open…" Aura Lee was breathing faster, and her cheeks were bloodless.

Noreen's color was little better. "*Fingers* came out of the *tray*?" She and Rose exchanged an appalled look.

"F-fingers were transparent and the shrieking was so loud that I couldn't, I couldn't—"

Rose sloshed brandy into her cup and shoved it toward her. Aura Lee swallowed it down and her labored breathing eased.

Noreen rubbed her arms, still trying to get warm. "I heard those sounds. Something not of this world was in that room with Aura Lee."

Rose shivered. "What are we up against? I thought, after Andrea, everything was going to be okay. But these, these *manifestations* are more terrifying than before, like something's growing stronger."

"It didn't start with Andrea." Aura Lee said with certainty. "It was when Cottie died. I've known since then that she's here and she's trying to tell us something."

The lines on Noreen's face had deepened. "Are you saying the thing that made those sounds is Caldicott Wyntham?" Her voice shook. "That she's the one who is—who is—"

"Haunting Wisdom Court?" Rose rubbed her forehead. "What are we going to do?"

Tears tracked down Aura Lee's cheeks. "I don't know if it's Cottie doing these things. She was—is— my friend. She was never anything but kind to me." She looked miserable. "I'm so *afraid* during these visitations. Twice now I've been so scared I couldn't accomplish anything." She dug for a tissue in her caftan pocket. "What's the point of trying to contact her if I fall apart when she shows up?"

Rose let out a deep sigh. "The sounds I heard coming from your room would terrify anybody. They scared the hell out of me. How can you maintain your cool when you're up against something like that, something so abnormal?" She leaned against the back of the chair, face weary. "I don't suppose you'd be willing to stop trying to contact Caldicott. The toll on our nerves is getting pretty steep."

"She has a point," Noreen agreed. "I can't imagine wanting to keep up your efforts after this."

With effort Aura Lee propelled herself off the sofa. "It's important that you listen to me. *I didn't try to contact Cottie.* I was reading a book I borrowed from a friend. It has a section about summoning spirits, but I didn't act on it. I didn't do *anything*. Whatever it was didn't need my help to appear."

"You mean whatever did that—the sounds and the fingers through the tray…" Noreen's voice died.

"Was acting on its own." Aura Lee glanced from Noreen to Rose, eyes filled with fear. "We need to find someone to help us. I can't deal with whatever is doing these things. I don't know if it's trying to tell us something or if it means us harm. I'm scared." She made her way to the bathroom. The click of the lock was loud in the hushed room.

Rose and Noreen looked at each other in dismay.

CHAPTER 12

———— ◆ ————

Cold water trickled down Kerry's neck and her eyes shot open. The blurry figure filling her vision sharpened into Max, who frowned down at her. He shifted the sopping washcloth in his hand to the floor, trailing drops across her shirt. "Are you all right?"

Kerry's eyelids drifted shut as she tried to figure out why she was lying on the living room rug.

"Can you hear me? Kerry, answer me!"

"Yeah." Her voice sounded far away, even to herself. "What's going on?" she added with more force. She stirred, and Max held out his hand to her. She grasped it, and he pulled her to her feet.

"Come sit down." His arm was solid around her shoulders as he guided her to the sofa, bracing her as she sank onto it.

Kerry's ears were buzzing, and her head floated somewhere near the ceiling. "Did I pass out?"

"Yes." Max examined her and then looked around the room in irritation. "Do you have any spirits—brandy, whiskey?"

Kerry riffled slowly through her scattered thoughts. "What?" she murmured. "You didn't like the tea?"

"Oh, for God's sake." Max bent over her, one hand lifting her chin until her eyes looked into his. "Not for me—for you. You just fainted! I'm trying to revive you."

With some difficulty Kerry focused on his face. He looked...harried, that was the word. "In the kitchen, maybe." Max straightened and headed out of the room, his limp pronounced.

Kerry shut her eyes. She could hear cabinet doors slamming. Evidently Max was having a hard time finding any booze. This pleased her for some reason, and a smile curved her lips. But as the fuzziness in her mind subsided, the smile died. She'd been making the tea...they'd been talking about Caldicott.

He'd found that piece of paper. Kerry shuddered. The writing was Caldicott's, no doubt about that. The paper was something she'd never seen before. Where *could* it have come from?

Max came back into the room, bottle in one hand, teacup in the other. "Drink this." He held out the cup.

Her nose wrinkled at the fumes as she took it. She considered the cup with suspicion. "What is it?"

"Slivovitz." Max looked impatient at her grimace of distaste. "Don't blame me, it's all I could find. If you hate it so much, why do you have the stuff?"

"It's not mine. Somebody left it behind."

"In any event, drink it down." When she didn't immediately comply, he growled, "Drink it!"

"Okay. Jeez." Kerry put the cup to her mouth and tossed back the clear liquid. It burned all the way down her throat, and heat radiated through her chest. She coughed miserably.

The lines across Max's brow eased as she sat up straighter. "That appears to have done the trick."

Kerry shuddered at kick of the alcohol. "Ugh, it's awful. What's it made of, lighter fluid?"

"Plums." Max removed the cup from her grasp and set it onto the coffee table. He sat down, turning toward her. "Now that you're back amongst the living, I want to know what just occurred."

Kerry slumped back into the sofa cushion, closing her eyes again at the stern note in his voice. "Why do you always sound like you're wearing a three-piece suit?"

"I beg your pardon."

Wincing at the umbrage in his voice, Kerry sighed. "Never mind. As to *what just occurred*, I am damned if I know."

He searched her face, clearly unsettled. "Do you mean you don't remember, or—"

"I remember." Kerry leaned forward, resting her head in her hands. "I mean I don't know what happened. I don't know where that paper came from." She turned toward him. "I don't know how in the world that scrap of paper got into the book—your book. Is that clear enough for you?"

Max scowled. "That doesn't make any sense."

"Ya think?" Kerry sighed. "I don't even know where to start to make sense of this. It's like I told you, I've been beating my brains out trying to find anything I could about Caldicott's personal life." She waved a hand in a defeated gesture. "Brick walls, Max, nothing but brick walls. And today, out of a book I'd been reading as recently as *yesterday* comes a page torn out of something else, and it has Caldicott's handwriting on it." She shook her head helplessly. "It beats the hell out of me, Max. No kidding."

"Well." Max sat for a moment, and she wondered what he was thinking. He reached for the bottle of slivovitz, and carefully refilled the teacup. He set the bottle on the table and swallowed the contents of the cup all in one go.

Kerry was obscurely pleased at his convulsive gasp.

"Bollocks," he croaked when he was able to speak. "That's gruesome."

Kerry nodded morosely. "Yeah."

The scent of pine teased Brenna's nose. The sluggish afternoon air had been pushed east by the twilight breeze sliding among the trees, rustling through the brush along the trail. Day's end edged the hills above her, casting tree-shadow fingers pulling the hillside toward the deepening gloom. She snapped a shot, hoping she'd get at least a suggestion of the effect, wishing for her sixteen-millimeter camera with its wider lens. *That's what I get for using the digital to scout the lay of the land.* The flash on her camera blinked, the light disappearing into the dusk.

She turned back toward Wisdom Court. She'd already spent a couple of hours with her own thoughts after the fiasco at Images and Dreams. If she went to the communal dinner, she'd have to talk to the others, and making chitchat would be more work than it was worth.

The longer she thought about seeing stars swirling in the ocean waves in her film, the more ridiculous it became. God, she'd sounded like an idiot telling whatshisname about it. She was lucky he hadn't called the nearest mental health center.

Brenna realized she was panting for breath, and stopped at the edge of Baseline Road to rest. A slab of granite roughened with lichen caught her eye, and she snapped several shots. Up close the scalloped edges of the gray-green growth resembled an alien forest, and she considered using it as a special effect. A shrill bird cry split the air and when her gaze swung upward, she could see a hawk on the hunt for its evening meal.

Dink had asked her what she was smoking when she told him about the altered film. He knew she hadn't touched weed since before her grandmother died. But the whole thing did sound like either a bad dream or a bad trip. Gyrating stars, for God's sake—those would've been weird enough all by themselves. But then she'd gone and added the mystery of the mythical fortune cookie. Her cheeks burned. Talking about it out loud only made her look stupid. Irritably she took several shots of a stand of pines crowding the edge of Gregory Creek.

Brenna heard footsteps behind her, along with heavy breathing. She turned sharply as a runner pounded past her, his flashlight shooting a cone of brightness over the trail. She watched the light bounce along as he thundered into the shadows ahead of her. It was getting dark faster than she'd realized. Hikers chatting on the way down from the upper paths greeted her as they passed her on the road beside the creek. The breeze had picked up, and the cooling edge of it brought out goose bumps on her arms. Dying grasses on the hillside waved slowly in reminder that winter would arrive before long. Out across the valley she could see the lights of Boulder flickering like fireflies.

By the time she reached the Wisdom Court boundary, Brenna was shivering. She sidled through the break in the hedge around the yard, her footsteps silent on the grass. Wood smoke drifted through fluttering aspen leaves, and the acrid scent reminded her of childhood campfires and ghost stories whispered in defiance of surrounding darkness. She paused to aim the camera at the main house. It might already be too dark to pick up much, but she hadn't taken any shots of the back of the house. She walked across the yard, pausing again to take an angled shot of the attic window high above her.

She glanced over her shoulder, pinpricks of awareness tingling between her shoulder blades. Something was in the dark with her. She increased her pace, her eyes straining to see the lawn's surface, on the alert for any obstacles.

She was nearly running when she rounded the side of the house. The electric lanterns above the doors of the two associate houses, as well as the yard lights along the fountain at the center of the circular driveway, illuminated the cobblestone expanse. The murmur of the water and the thud of her shoes against the bricks were the only sounds.

Swiftly Brenna leapt up the steps to her building, key in hand. Moments later she was jerking open the door to her flat, slipping inside, turning the latch. The reach for the light switch was instinctive. In the silent living room she heard her rapid breathing and felt the pounding of her heart. What had just happened? She was frightened, but of what? She'd seen no one, had heard nothing threatening.

Brenna went to the sofa and settled onto it. As she put her camera onto the coffee table, it rattled against the glass top, and she saw her hands were trembling. Had it been a panic attack or had she'd picked up on something wrong?

Slowly her breathing evened and she stopped shaking. Pushing herself off the sofa, she went to the kitchen. When she faced the bank of uncovered windows, she stopped in the doorway. *Dammit, stop acting like a scared kid!* She hurried to the cabinet over the counter and yanked a glass off the shelf. Tugging at the cork, she tilted the Bailey's bottle over the glass, knocking it against the rim only twice before the glass was full. Turning her back on the blank panes, she snatched up the bottle. When she reached the living room, her hands were trembling again. She gulped a healthy swig of the liqueur.

Brenna set down the glass and bottle, then sank onto the couch, snagging the green plaid throw from the arm, wrapping it around her shoulders. She didn't have to think about it right now. Probably be better if she didn't. *Too much weird shit going on.* She fumbled for the camera, nearly knocking it off the coffee table before she curled her fingers around it. She'd gotten some shots—enough to warrant going back with the sixteen-millimeter. The lighting would be a bitch to get right, but it'd be worth it to try.

Flicking the switch to run back through the photos she'd taken, she reached again for the glass. Sipping the creamy liqueur, she saw a decent snap of the lichen on the rock, and a stand of pine saplings that wasn't too bad. She'd caught the look of interdependence in the way the spindly young trees leaned against each other, as if too many strong winds had come their way.

When she came to the image of the finger-shadows extending down the hill, Brenna sighed. No way could the small lens capture the impression of claws, but she'd hoped for more than she'd gotten. The dark areas dominated the square screen, with the trees themselves showing up as only lighter vertical shapes. The flash had illuminated the nearest trunks, but that served to focus on the pines rather than the shadows. How would she manage the contrast?

She moved on to the shots of the house. Her gaze sharpened. A whitish shape was under the roofline, near the attic window. Brenna gently rubbed against the screen with a corner of the throw, but she couldn't make out what it was. No way to tell without more detail. She levered herself off the sofa and headed for the studio and her laptop.

Downloading the snapshots onto the hard drive, Brenna sipped more of the liqueur. She was feeling better. Nothing like a little alcohol to even out the bumps. Bumps in the night, no, things that go bump in the night.

Glancing down at the laptop screen, Brenna saw the download had been completed. She clicked through the shots, stopping at the series she'd taken of Wisdom Court. Another click enlarged them, and she bent over the first shot to check for the anomaly. There it was. She jerked back in shock, and the glass slipped out of her hand onto the rug. "Holy shit."

A chill snaked down her spine. She was looking at a white face in the attic window. From it desperate eyes stared at her.

CHAPTER 13

The upstairs hall was shrouded in afternoon shadows, and Rose wished she'd turned on the overhead light near the back stairs. Since the other switch was at the end of the corridor, she could either go back or continue toward her room. Moving forward, she heard the thirteen chimes of the grandfather clock on the first floor. Dinner would be soon, and they would talk about what had been happening at Wisdom Court. With any luck someone would have some ideas. Maybe Brenna would be a source of new information. In California they probably dealt with troubled spirits all the time. Of course, from what she read, most of *them* were still alive.

She saw the door to Caldicott's room was ajar. Curious, she walked nearer, and peeked inside. In the gloom something moved and she inhaled sharply.

"Is that you, Rose?" It was Aura Lee.

With a sigh of relief, Rose pushed open the door. Aura Lee sat on the edge of the chaise longue, her shoulders slumped, one hand stroking Strudel. The little dachshund's head rested on her paws, and her eyes were closed in bliss. Aura Lee had changed into a deep purple caftan that announced mourning as clearly as her lost expression. "She was scratching at the door to be let in," she said. "We've been sitting here together."

"I'm sorry." Rose flicked the light switch and crossed the Oriental rug, brushing against the flowered duvet on the canopy bed. She sat down beside Aura Lee and took her hand, patting it in sympathy. Strudel opened one eye and closed it again. "It's been a hard day."

Aura Lee nodded. "A dreadful day." They were silent for a long moment.

Strudel sat up suddenly, ears at attention. Aura Lee sighed deeply. "I've been thinking all afternoon. I'm afraid I might have set something in motion, but I swear I don't know what it is." Beside her Strudel had begun to growl deep in her throat.

Rose frowned at the dog. "Now what?"

Strudel leapt off the chaise and made a beeline for the fireplace, all the while barking madly.

"What is it? Strudel, stop it!" They stood up to go after her, but Strudel yipped and began backing away from the fireplace. Her barks died into whines, and she began to howl.

They both bent to grab her, but a scraping noise jerked their attention to the fireplace. The beveled mirror hanging above it slipped down the wall, struck the mantel, and smashed onto the hearth. "No!" Aura Lee cried in horror. "Not Cottie's mirror."

"Watch out for glass." Rose picked up Strudel, now whimpering piteously, and felt her trembling.

Aura Lee murmured in distress as she examined the wall where the looking glass had hung. "What caused it to fall? The hook is right there. Oh, it was so lovely. Cottie said a dear friend gave it to her years ago."

"Hush, baby, hush," Rose murmured to Strudel. The little dog was whining, still quivering. Rose carried her to the door. "I'm going to put her out in the hall so she won't get cut. I don't know what's wrong with her."

Rose set Strudel down, and she barked once. Then she trotted along the carpet runner to the back stairs and started down. "Weird." Rose returned to Caldicott's room. "She went downstairs as if nothing had happened."

Aura Lee was picking up pieces of glass and putting them in the wastebasket from beside the bed. "It's such a shame."

Rose bent to help and glimpsed metal mixed among the glass fragments. She used a piece of the frame to push aside bits of glass, uncovering a small container the size of a pillbox. Carefully she picked it up and rested it on her palm. It was made of silver with a hinge on one side.

"What do you have there?" asked Aura Lee. She peered at it over Rose's shoulder as she tried to find a way open it. "It must've been attached to the mirror somehow."

Rose slid her thumbnail under the narrow lip of the lid, and felt something inside give way. She heard the barest click, and the top swung open. Inside was a twist of paper, and a small brass key slipped from it when she pulled it from the box. She tilted the key onto her palm.

Aura Lee drew closer. "What in the world could it be for?"

"A jewelry case, a safety deposit box. Who knows? The paper is blank." Rose glanced down at the floor. "Do you see anything else that might've been with it?"

Aura Lee craned to look more closely at the remains

of the mirror but found nothing. "Wouldn't there be the name of a bank if it were a safety deposit box?" At Rose's shrug, she said, "It's so frustrating! There's no way to know what it might unlock."

"Another mystery. Just what we need." Rose put the key back into the box. As she started to close the lid, the light from the ceiling fixture shone on the inner surface. "Wait a minute." Rose slanted it toward the fixture to get a better look. "Huh. It looked as though something was scratched out." She peered at the crude marks. "But something's been cut over that. I think it's a circle, or maybe an 'O'."

"A circle?" Aura Lee fumbled with her glasses hanging at her neck and peered into the box. "You're right. Like the circles around your fountain dishes," she said pointedly.

"I doubt that." Rose slipped the box into her pocket, her attention shifting to the mess on the floor. "I guess we'd better get this cleaned up. I'm glad nobody got hurt from it. Who knows how long it's been ready to drop off the wall."

"I know. I suppose the hanger could've been defective, but it looks okay." Aura Lee brushed past her, and stopped. "What's that on the rug?" She stooped to examine it more closely. "Is that blood?" She glanced at Rose. "Oh, no. You're bleeding."

"What?" Rose lifted her hand and saw blood dripping from it to the floor. "It doesn't even hurt."

Aura Lee tut-tutted, snatching a tissue from the bedside table. "Here. Hold it tightly to stop the bleeding. We'll have to make sure there isn't any glass in the cut. You know how tiny some of those splinters can be."

Rose wrapped her finger. "It'll be all right." She glanced down at the wool Oriental. Among shards of glass, next to the woven pattern of a Chinese dog, was a ring-shaped bloodstain. "I hope I didn't ruin the rug. I'll get something to wash it out."

When she returned with a spray bottle of stain remover, Rose found the bloodstain had expanded into the pattern of the rug. The blot was a perfect, pitch-black circle.

Rose turned away from the knowing look on Aura Lee's face.

CHAPTER 14

With darkness had come a cold wind. The bare cottonwood branches creaked like rusty hinges. Shadows leapt around the Wisdom Court buildings, trying to get to the light inside.

Andrea clutched her unbuttoned jacket to her chest and ran up the main house steps. From the driveway came the tap-tap of Neal's pickup horn, and she spun to wave, fumbling with the latch behind her. The door swung open and she stumbled inside, nearly flattening Noreen. Together they leaned against the door to defeat the gust shoving in behind her.

"Wow! It's getting nasty out there." Andrea shrugged out of her coat and hung it on one of the hooks beside the stairs. "Think it'll snow?"

"It could." Noreen's gaze went to the windows. "I've heard it's even snowed here in August."

Andrea shivered. "At least we missed that. Let's hope not in September, either. I'd have to get some warmer clothes."

"You'll probably have to do that anyway. Last winter had some downright bone-chilling days." Noreen led the way toward the dining room, elegant in a magenta sweater and rustling black skirt. "And Boulder gets more wind than any other place I've lived."

Andrea made a face at the thought, but any concerns regarding weather disappeared as she paused in the arched doorway.

The dining room was inviting, candles grouped along the middle of the long walnut table, the brass light fixture lustrous overhead. The centerpiece bouquet of dried red and gold leaves was reflected in the sideboard mirror along with the crystal decanters filled with brandy and port. The air was fragrant with pot roast and bay leaf, with an underlying hint of brownies just taken out of the oven.

Andrea inhaled deeply and smiled in pleasure. "What's the occasion?"

Kerry came through from the kitchen carrying a massive wooden salad bowl, pausing to let the door swing shut against her hip. "We'll find out, won't we?" Her green sweater set off her pale skin and auburn hair. She found a place for the bowl and pulled out a chair to sit down.

Andrea inspected her more closely. Had she been crying? Lately her inability to trace Caldicott's background had shadowed everything. Had she encountered more difficulties?

"It's the usual Thursday dinner." Rose entered from the hallway carrying a bottle of wine in each hand. She gestured with the Chablis Blanc. "Sit. Aura Lee's bringing in the pièce de résistance. You want white or red?"

Something's off with her, too. Andrea saw that Rose's fixed smile didn't reach her eyes. "What's the red?"

Rose glanced at the bottle. "Shiraz. Australian."

"That's for me, thanks." Andrea reached for the

gray cotton napkin beside the heavy flatware. As Rose filled her glass, Brenna slid into place beside her and scooted her chair closer to the table.

"Hi." Brenna cast a glance at Rose, who was filling Noreen's glass. "Any idea what's going on?" she asked in a low voice. "I wasn't going to come tonight, but Rose practically put a gun to my head."

Andrea shrugged. "She'll let us know." She regarded the younger woman with concern. The dark circles under Brenna's eyes made her wonder when she'd last slept. She wore an olive shirt that gave her complexion a sickly tinge.

The door to the kitchen swung open, and Aura Lee carried in a platter with pot roast surrounded by yams and sautéed pearl onions, broccoli florets, and strips of red peppers. Chunks of celery and whole mushrooms lay at each end. She nodded at their appreciative murmurs, and went back to the kitchen, returning with a smaller plate she set in front of Brenna.

"Roast seitan. Thanks." Brenna flashed a smile. "I'm a vegetarian," she explained, pointing at the meat-like substance in a nest of vegetables.

"Is that like tofu?" asked Noreen.

"It's made of grains. I like it better than the soy in tofu, although some tofu dishes can be great." Brenna stopped and fumbled with her fork. "I'm babbling."

"Wouldn't be the first time that's happened around here." Kerry spooned yams onto her plate, and turned the platter in Andrea's direction. The others filled their plates and glasses. Conversation ebbed as they began to eat.

"This is so good," Andrea said after a while. "There's a reason they call it home cooking, Aura Lee."

"Isn't that the truth?" Noreen surveyed her plate

with pleasure. "If I were a better person, I'd feel guilty that I always buy takeout when it's my turn to supply food. But I'm not, and I don't." She took another bite.

"Oh, now, it's just a roast." Aura Lee moved some broccoli around on her plate and smiled mechanically.

"What did she mean about her turn to supply food?" Brenna asked Andrea in a low voice.

What had happened to Aura Lee's energy and enthusiasm? "What?" Andrea glanced at Brenna and caught up with the question. "Oh, didn't Rose tell you? The group dinners are every Thursday, and we take turns providing the meal so Aura Lee doesn't get stuck with all the cooking."

"Tell her what?" Rose hadn't eaten much more than Aura Lee. "What have I forgotten now?"

"The thing about taking turns with Thursday dinners."

Rose sighed. "I'm sorry. So much has been going on, I spaced it out. It's no big deal," she assured Brenna. "You can do what Noreen does, and order take-out. It's turned into a tradition over the years that we share responsibility for that one meal."

Brenna nodded. "I can do that. Maybe I'll get up enough nerve to make my pasta Alfredo. It's pretty good."

Noreen stabbed a piece of celery from the platter. "I've been trained to eat anything. The cooks at a private girls' school," she explained to Brenna. "You wouldn't believe some of the things I've been served."

Without warning Aura Lee sniffed mightily, and pushed away from the table, fumbling at her sleeve for the tissue tucked inside it. "Excuse me, please," she said in a muffled voice. She hurried toward the kitchen.

The women around the table exchanged puzzled glances.

"I'll go." Rose disappeared through the swinging door.

Noreen looked after her in dismay. "I was trying to pay her a compliment, not compare her to the school cooks. I don't know why she would've misunderstood." Then her mouth snapped shut, and her eyes widened as a thought struck her.

"She seems upset." Andrea paused. "Am I the only who's picking up on some strange vibes tonight?"

Kerry put down her fork. "I don't know what's up with Aura Lee, but I had a weird thing happen today." She reached for her wineglass. "I'm still freaked out about it."

Noreen nodded. *"And when strange follows upon the singular, what was familiar becomes foreign, and no comfort is to be had in what is known.* Prudence Whilom Evans, 1849-1884."

Andrea thought how devastating events would have to be to cause that degree of detachment from one's own life. She registered the years mentioned. "Civil War?"

"Confederate side." Noreen surveyed her dinner partners, taking shrewd measure of their uneasiness. "Perhaps we've all encountered some mysteries of late."

"Yes, and we need to talk about them." Rose reentered the dining room from the hallway. Aura Lee followed her, dabbing at her damp eyes with a handkerchief. The others traded quick glances as the two resumed their places.

Rose refilled her glass and fidgeted with her silverware. When she looked up from the table, her expression was grim. "I planned to wait until after dinner, but since you've already brought it up, let's talk now." She glanced at Aura Lee. "Today presented a tipping point for Wisdom Court. We might as well lay it all out so we all know where we stand."

Andrea felt a shiver down her back. "I don't like the sound of that."

Rose's troubled gray eyes flicked toward her. "You know the kinds of things going on over the last few months. What happened with you..." Her voice trailed off.

"You mean the haunting you described, right?" Brenna asked.

Rose took a deep breath. "Yes, the haunting." She picked up her wineglass and set it back down. "What took place today convinced me Wisdom Court is still haunted. I thought after Andrea's experience we'd laid the ghosts to rest, but there've been so many strange things since then." She stared at her plate. "I don't know how else to explain them."

"What do you mean, exactly?" Brenna looked from Rose to Aura Lee. "You talked about Andrea's experiences before. Has something else happened? Have you actually seen ghosts?"

Rose moved uncomfortably in her chair and Noreen responded, "Not seen, heard."

"When did this happen?"

Noreen paid no attention to Kerry's exclamation. "Today I heard something I *hope* was a ghost. I don't even want to imagine what it could've been if it wasn't."

"Come on, spill it," Kerry said.

Rose described the shrieking noise from Aura Lee's room that afternoon. "It was a hideous sound, so loud we could hardly hear Aura Lee calling for help. We had to force open the door to get her out."

"Did you *see* anything?" Andrea heard the quaver in her voice and cleared her throat.

"I did not." Noreen's shoulders moved in a tiny shrug. "However—"

"I saw something incredible," Aura Lee said. "Something impossible. Fingers were extending up from the surface of my silver tray. They were transparent, starting to reach for the perfume bottles there."

Kerry just looked at them. Finally she said slowly, "If it weren't for what happened with Andrea, I'd have to think all three of you are batshit crazy."

"Oh, Kerry, if you'd heard it…it was so appalling." Noreen shared a grim look with Rose. "Whatever was making that noise could've done anything."

"Couldn't it have been an hallucination? You were doing another spell, right?" Kerry's gaze veered back to Aura Lee. "Those herbs you use could've made you see illusions, could've made any damn thing look plausible."

Aura Lee shook her head. "It happened."

"That's what scared me the most." Rose folded her hands on the table. "Aura Lee said she was reading. The fingers, the sounds all occurred on their own."

Andrea felt the hollowness in her stomach. She'd almost forgotten her dread at what had overcome her after her arrival in Boulder. Every time she'd picked up a paintbrush or a pencil, she wasn't sure she would be the one using it. The old fear slipped back into place as if it had never left her.

"Let me get this straight." Brenna bent toward Aura Lee in fascination. "This hand you saw came up from a tray?"

Aura Lee nodded. "Lights moved around on the surface, like on a pond, and the hand was pushing until the fingers broke through and came up among the colors. There was a humming sound that kept getting louder until I couldn't stand it."

"That's even weirder than what I saw." Brenna smiled crookedly. "I was snapping pictures outside this house last night and when I checked later, I found a shot of someone looking out of the attic window."

"Dear God," Noreen muttered. "What is happening here?" Her worried expression intensified. "It's as if someone's pushed an 'on' button for spookiness."

Andrea reached for her wine. She pretended her hand wasn't shaking. "Brenna, could you see *who* was looking out the window? Was it a blonde woman?" She emptied her glass.

"I couldn't tell. It was a sad, lost face." Brenna swallowed. "It was almost like it was asking me for help."

"Oh, man." Kerry let out a breath. "My scary stuff can't compete with yours or Aura Lee's, even though I passed out because of it."

"What?" The lines on Rose's face deepened. "Tell us."

"Max offered to help me hunt for more info about Caldicott. While I was checking his background, I got a copy of a book he wrote." She saw the glance between Rose and Noreen. "I couldn't take him at face value without digging a little bit. Anyway, I've had that book for the last week, and I read the whole thing." Her voice trailed off.

"And?" Noreen asked pointedly.

Kerry said in a rush, "We were at my place. The book—his book—fell on the floor. A piece of paper slipped out of it, a fragment of one of Caldicott's journals. One I've never seen."

Aura Lee made a shocked sound, her hand flying to her mouth. "A message from Cottie?"

"Not a message. It was from the title page from a journal dated nineteen thirty-nine to nineteen forty-five, written in Caldicott's hand. And I've never found anything that old, nothing." Kerry's hands clenched. "I'd give anything to get hold of that journal."

"Where could it have come from?" Rose asked blankly.

"That's the question." Kerry slumped in her chair. "Though maybe it's a dangerous one to ask."

"So you fainted?" Brenna asked in curiosity. "When you found it, I mean."

"Yeah." Kerry's lips twitched reluctantly. "Just like the heroine of a gothic novel."

"And did Max resuscitate you?" Noreen's voice was dry.

Kerry dropped her hand back to the table. Her cheeks were pink. "He was actually pretty nice about it."

"But where did the fragment come from?" demanded Rose.

"*The Mystery of the Appearing Fragment*," murmured Brenna, her eyes bright with interest. "I can't compete with my *Mystery of the Odd Fortune Cookie*."

This surprised a laugh from Noreen. "Sorry, it's so Agatha Christie. What do you mean?"

Brenna described the adventure with her take-out Chinese dinner. "I threw the fortune away, but when I went to the kitchen to look for my phone, it was back on the table." She dug in her jeans pocket and pulled out a small piece of paper and handed it to Andrea.

"Kind acts result in new friends," Andrea read aloud.

"Bland enough, right?" Brenna took back the paper. "But when I first read it, what I saw written over it were the words *Behind circle*, like someone had scrawled it with a pencil. When I looked at it the second time, those words were gone. I was weirded out because I thought somebody might be playing a trick on me, so I there I was, checking the locks and looking into closets." She caught sight of Rose's expression. "What wrong? You look like you've just see a ghost."

The overhead light blinked off as air gusted through the room, blowing out every candle. It was utterly dark.

"What the hell!"

That was Kerry. Rose found the table edge and held on as she stood up. "Noreen, can you find the switch?"

"I'm closer," said Andrea. Patting sounds followed. "Ouch!"

"Why's it so damned dark?" Kerry snapped. "Is it a blackout?"

A thump was followed by a click and the lights came on. Andrea lowered her hand from the light switch as Rose sat down.

Aura Lee shrieked, pointing at the table.

"What is it?"

"My God," Brenna murmured.

Rose followed her gaze. The serving platter was empty and every dinner plate on the table had around it a circle formed with pieces of yams and celery, mushrooms and broccoli, pepper strips and pearl onions. The remains of the roast were arranged around the vase of autumn leaves.

CHAPTER 15

They fled to the living room and clustered together in the dim light of the lamp in the corner. "What just happened?" Andrea asked in a wobbly voice.

"I don't know but I don't want it to happen again." Kerry rubbed her arms, hunched against the chill in the room. "That took about ten years off my life."

"What if it comes in here?" Aura Lee whispered.

Noreen glanced around. "Maybe it already has." As the color drained from Aura Lee's cheeks, she quickly added, "No, no, I'm sure that's not the case. We're safe in here because the…entity probably used up all its energy rearranging our dinner."

Brenna couldn't suppress a laugh, but it sounded almost hysterical, even to her.

Kerry made a beeline for the fireplace and pushed the switch to turn on the blue and yellow flames.

Brenna was cold to the bone. *Heat is a good idea.* She hurried to the warmth on trembling legs and the others followed.

"Thanks, Kerry." Rose sounded shaky, but she picked up a throw from the sofa and set it around Aura Lee's shoulders and checked the others to see how they were doing.

Brenna rubbed her hands together in front of the blaze and turned to thaw the chunk of ice that was her spine. Right in front of her were the naked windowpanes with a view of the trees behind the house. The windblown branches looked like arms flailing against the night. She overcame her dread long enough to approach the glass and find the drapery cord. She tugged on it and the rich burgundy curtains surged together, shutting out the battle. When she saw Kerry staring at her she said defiantly, "I don't like the dark."

"Me, neither," said Kerry. "Not tonight."

Rose had Aura Lee settled and now motioned to the others to sit down. Brenna was turning on every light fixture in the room and passing out more throws and blankets. If they were warm, she thought, maybe they could think clearly about what to do next.

Aura Lee stiffened. "What's that?"

Brenna heard a high-pitched whine.

Kerry turned her head toward the door to the kitchen. "Is it Strudel?" She glanced around the room. "She wasn't in the dining room, was she?"

"No." The lines on Aura Lee's face deepened with worry. "She's alone in my place."

"She'd better be alone," Rose muttered. They exchanged glances.

"I really don't want to leave this room." Brenna's memory flashed an image of Strudel wagging her tail as she licked her hand. *She's a sweet little dog. Dammit.*

"Yeah," Andrea said. "She's probably okay."

Kerry glared at the fire. "I guess I could go get her."

I can only die once. "I'll race you." Brenna jumped to her feet and took the lead, Kerry right behind her.

Brenna slowed down when she saw the kitchen

lights were out. The square windows over the sink reflected their movements.

"I don't know why I'm so scared." Kerry sounded breathless as they trailed past the refrigerator.

"You're kidding, right?" Brenna cast a quick glance around the shadowy cupboards and counters. The hanging pots gave her a bad moment, but she swallowed the gasp of fright. "It looks okay, I guess."

"Yeah." Kerry headed for the door to Aura Lee's quarters and grasped the knob. As she turned it, Strudel let loose a flurry of barks. "It's us, you silly dog." She pushed the door open and light spilled from the room. She stepped inside just as the cabinet organ in the corner droned a single note. Brenna bumped into her, forcing her further into the room.

"Shit!" Kerry scooped up the dog and turned to run as Brenna backed up to give her space.

Brenna looked at the organ and her heart skipped when she saw the candelabra candles begin to burn. At the same time some of the organ keys sank in a loud chord. The volume increased slowly.

"Oh-God, oh-God, oh-God." Kerry clutched Strudel to her chest and plunged out the door, Brenna at her heels. They ran across the kitchen and into the living room, pulling the swinging door shut behind them.

"What is it?" Andrea demanded. "What happened?"

Brenna waved a hand toward the door. "In Aura Lee's room—the organ—candles lit—I saw the keys—something pressed on the keys. Didn't you hear it?"

"Look out!"

Aura Lee lurched to one side, eyes closed, in danger of sliding off the sofa. Rose grabbed her by the arm and Andrea pulled her up against the back cushions. "Maybe we should get her lying down."

Kerry set down Strudel and helped Rose shift and

turn Aura Lee's legs as Andrea got a pillow for her head. "Poor thing," Andrea murmured. "This has been so hard on her."

"Not just her." Noreen bent over Aura Lee and took her hand. "Aura Lee, wake up," she said in a louder voice, patting her hand. "Everything is all right, my dear. We need you to join us now. Get her a glass of water, will you?"

Aura Lee stirred and her eyes fluttered. "Mama's organ," she whispered. She opened her eyes and looked at Noreen and then at Andrea. "Why am I lying down?" Confused, she accepted Andrea's hand to sit up and took the glass from Rose. In a few minutes she looked stronger, although her face was far more pale than usual. When Strudel jumped up beside her, she stroked the dog with a trembling hand.

"Where were we?" Rose asked and appeared surprised when Brenna and Kerry laughed, albeit shakily.

"When we were so rudely interrupted?" Kerry took a deep breath and let it out in tremulous sigh. "You didn't hear the organ, did you?"

"No." Rose glanced at Noreen. "Did you? Or you?" she asked Andrea. They both shook their heads.

"God, it was spooky." Brenna shivered. "There was a full-out *Phantom of the Opera* chord, and it was getting louder as we ran out. How could so much sound have been confined to that single room?"

"Did you see anything?" Noreen asked. "Did anything materialize?"

"No, I didn't. You?" Kerry asked Brenna.

"Just the candles on the organ. They started burning while I was watching. The lights were already on, so maybe we couldn't see who was playing."

"Ugh. There's a thought." Rose glanced at the coffee table, and then the end tables when she didn't find what she was looking for. "Do we have any paper in here? Something to write with?"

The others searched the room, and finally Andrea found a tablet in a drawer in the liquor cabinet. "Here. What's it for?"

"I want to write down everything we talk about so we can keep track of what's going on. Otherwise we'll never figure out what we're dealing with."

"I hope we can," Kerry muttered. "It's such a mess." Her gaze lit on the bottles. "I want some of that."

"Brandy?" Noreen shook her head. "Let's wait until we've debriefed each other. Rose is right. We have to keep track of these *visitations,* for lack of a better word. Things are heating up around here and if we're to do anything about them, we need to know what we're up against."

Rose looked up from the paper where she'd begun a list. "Let's start with the dining room. Everything seemed normal to me until the lights went out. What about the rest of you? Do you recall anything that might have triggered our...guest?"

Aura Lee shuddered at the word, but said nothing.

Kerry's eyes narrowed in the effort to remember. "We were talking about strange things happening to us, like the title page from Caldicott's journal and Brenna's stars in her film. And the fortune cookie."

"Yeah, that was when the lights went out," Brenna said. "Do you think it might be because we were comparing notes? Could that have made the, uh, the ghost angry?"

"But whose ghost?" Aura Lee's blue eyes were clouded with worry. "Say it was Cottie, then why would she *not* want us to talk about our experiences? It makes no sense."

"But if it's not Caldicott?" Noreen pursed her lips.

"What if we have someone else haunting Wisdom Court? Maybe multiple someones."

Rose continued writing. "For all we know, when Andrea sketched Kelvin Haslett during our first haunting, it lit up a welcome sign in the land of the dead and we've got spirits coming out the woodwork." At their silence, she glanced up at them. "Sorry. Every time I actually think about what we're saying, I want to run screaming from the room."

"I'll second that." Kerry rubbed her forehead. "Let's keep going. The dinner table decorations—the vegetables around the plates?" she added at Andrea's quizzical look. "That was a variation on Rose's fountains being taken apart. So again we've got circles, this time lots of them. And Brenna's fortune cookie said *behind circle*. What in the sweet hell can circles have to do with all this?"

Aura Lee sat a little straighter. "As I told Rose, the circle is an important symbol. It can mean a lot of things."

"And that's the problem." Rose drew a small circle on the paper. "You said it could be a door between worlds, that it could be a message from beyond, that it could stand for Circe's spinning wheel, for heavens sake. But which? And how are we supposed to know? Did you learn anything else in your research?"

Aura Lee looked at her hands. "Well, yes," she said reluctantly, "I learned a lot. The circle has many more meanings than I realized. It can represent eternity, life, the tree of life, the egg of life, protection—"

Kerry groaned. "What good does that do us? We could spend a year trying to nail down the right symbolic interpretation as Wisdom Court fills up with ghosts."

Into the discouraged silence Brenna said, "What about architecture? I mean, circles are used a lot in windows and doors, and in landscaping and such. What if these recurring circles have something to do with Wisdom Court itself?"

They all stared at her. Then Andrea said, admiration tingeing her voice, "That's a good idea. What if the repeated circles refer to something or some place right here?"

Rose narrowed her eyes as she thought. "Hmm, it's certainly worth considering. At the moment I can't think of anything architectural here involving circles, but that doesn't mean there isn't something." She looked at Brenna. "At least it gives us a starting point."

Noreen nodded judiciously. "'*The initial step of a journey has more importance than the last, for it determines the boundaries of exploration and thus defines the final chart of discovery.*' Lucinda Blythe Hartshorne, 1833 to 1901. An early explorer of the Amazon," she added.

"That's what we could use," Aura Lee pronounced. "An explorer! Someone who's familiar with the paranormal." She looked sadly at Rose. "I haven't been able to do much during these situations. I never thought I'd say it, but I don't have enough experience to deal with what's been happening."

Rose patted her shoulder. "Because you're personally involved," she said. "Like a doctor not being allowed to treat members of her own family. You and Caldicott were best friends, and it's hard for you to come up against these manifestations, thinking they might have something to do with her."

"They have taught me that I don't know enough. We need to find someone to guide us through this, someone who's used to contact with these spirits."

Rose looked around the group. "I'm willing if all of you are. We need to agree to any action we take."

"We're not talking about Belinda Smythe, are we?" Kerry still held a grudge against the medium who'd unsuccessfully conducted a séance to contact Caldicott Wyntham.

"No. We need someone who has a broader background in the field." Rose nodded encouragingly at Aura Lee. "Do you know of anyone who might help us?"

"I can put out feelers in the psychic community." Already Aura Lee was looking more herself. Her cheeks were pink, and her eyes were interested again.

Noreen smiled. "That would be helpful."

The front door bell chimed, startling them all. "Lord," Kerry said with feeling. "My nerves are shot to hell."

Rose was halfway across the room when Andrea said, "Wait, I'll come with you."

"Don't be silly." Rose kept moving toward the door. "Nothing's going to hurt me."

"Let her go with you," Noreen said. "We need to stick together."

The doorbell rang again.

"Oh, all right." Rose motioned to Andrea. "Come on then."

As they left the room, Kerry turned to Noreen. "Do you really think we're in any kind of danger?"

"I don't know, but we're already scared. I don't like the idea of any one of us going through the kind of terror Aura Lee had yesterday. Seeing that spirit hand groping, and hearing the hideous sounds in your room couldn't have been easy for you."

Aura Lee's lips tightened. "It's not knowing what to expect next that I find so frightening."

"That's why your suggestion about getting someone in here to help us is a good one," said Noreen. "If we can find a paranormalist, or whatever they're called, who can help us understand the signs we've seen, maybe we can resolve our haunting."

"*Seek and ye shall find,*" Rose said from the doorway. She stepped into the room and Brenna was intrigued by the expression on her face. Either she was irritated or taken aback.

Max Steadman followed Rose toward the sofa and Andrea slipped into her chair. "Max says he came because he felt that something is wrong here at Wisdom Court."

Aura Lee's gaze flew to his face. "What do you mean?" When he remained silent, she patted the sofa cushion beside her. "Come sit down."

Max made his way between chairs and settled onto the couch. His hair was windblown, and his coat unbuttoned. "I was reading after dinner—" Strudel climbed into his lap and he rubbed her ears. "I nodded off, and awoke abruptly some minutes later, convinced something was wrong here. When I telephoned, there was only a busy signal." He looked at each of them, eyes narrowing as his gaze stopped at Kerry. "I had to come."

The color rose in Kerry's cheeks, and her eyes softened. As Max smiled, she stiffened. "Wait a minute. You had a feeling something was wrong. And on the strength of that you came here."

"Sometimes I receive—that is—I have an awareness…" Max looked at Rose in appeal.

She sighed. "In addition to working as a genealogist, Max has just told me he's is a card-carrying member of the Royal Paranormal Society." Her smile was strained. "At least I assume there's an ID card."

CHAPTER 16

"The Royal Paranormal Society?" Kerry shook her head in confusion. "I don't understand."

"There was no reason to…" Max began, but Kerry interrupted him.

"So that's why you were so strange about the page from Caldicott's journal. You *wanted* it to be a ghost, right?" She pushed up out of her chair. "You fed me that lousy slivovitz and didn't say a word about being one of the supernatural patrol. Why didn't you tell me?"

"I'm sorry," Max said.

"I'm out of here." Kerry shot a glance at Rose. "Let me know when the expert has left." She got as far as the door when Max caught up with her.

He reached for her arm to stop her. "Let me explain."

Kerry sidestepped him. "You should've been up front when you got here, instead of spinning that yarn about searching for what's-her-name."

"I *am* searching for what's-her—The woman's name is Clara Trinder." By now Max, too, was yelling. "Do you have any idea how difficult it is to approach people and identify yourself as a paranormal investigator? You're fortunate if they don't show you the door with a boot at your backside to hurry you along."

"It's only what you deserve." Kerry folded her arms across her chest and lifted her chin. "How can you expect us to trust you when you lied to us?"

Noreen leaned closer to Rose. "Have you ever seen her like this?" she whispered.

Rose shook her head. "Nor him. So much for British reticence."

Andrea choked back a laugh, and Brenna murmured, "*Love Finds Andy Hardy.*"

"For the last time, I didn't lie," Max stated in glacial tones. "I just didn't tell you everything."

Kerry turned abruptly, fixing Brenna with a dirty look. "What did you say?"

"Who, me?" Brenna grinned at her. "Just talking about movies like I always do."

Rose cleared her throat. "The two of you obviously have a lot to talk about, but would you mind tabling it for now? I'd like to share our information while Max is here."

Kerry's face was flaming with color. "Sure, whatever." She flopped into the wingback chair. Silently Max pulled a chair over the rug so he could sit beside her.

"We can go into the details of your introduction some other time," Rose said. "For now, I'd like to hear more about this feeling you had tonight. What happened, exactly?"

Max rubbed his hand across his forehead. "As I said, I'd been reading and fell asleep. I was jerked awake suddenly. I felt there was danger nearby. My heart was pounding and I was at full alert." He looked at the sideboard. "I don't mean to be rude, but might I have a drink?" He slanted a look at Kerry.

Rose got to her feet. "We'd been waiting while we compared notes, but we can say it's medicinal." She glanced at the group. "Anyone else?"

"God, yes," Andrea said quickly. The others nodded.

Rose brought brandy and scotch to the low table and went back for glasses from the cabinet. "Thank goodness we have what we need here. I don't know if I'd be willing to brave the kitchen."

"Even for brownies?" Aura Lee said. "I baked them for dessert."

"Oh, man." Brenna had a pained expression. "Brownies."

Andrea pushed herself up from the sofa. "Ghost or no ghost, nobody's going to keep me from Aura Lee's brownies. I'll be back in a second." She strode toward the kitchen and pushed the swinging door open.

"Wait, I'll come, too," Kerry said to her back, but Andrea kept going.

"I'll go with her." Max got to his feet, but before he could get far, Andrea was back with a platter of the chocolate squares, and she set them on the coffee table.

"My hero." Brenna snatched a brownie and took a bite. "Oh, God, things look a lot better now." She chewed while she waited for Noreen to pour herself a drink, and then followed suit. "Anybody else want brandy?"

When everyone was supplied with refreshments, Rose nodded to Max. "Finish telling us."

He nodded. "As I told you, I woke convinced something was amiss, but everything appeared normal in the hotel room. Then, as I was attempting to make sense of it, I realized I was thinking quite strongly of Wisdom Court. Sometimes I have a mental image with these feelings," he added. "In my mind's eye I'll see a person or a place and the image will have a surrounding glow. This time I could see Wisdom Court. I could see you," he said to Kerry, his voice lower. "I knew you were in danger."

Kerry met his gaze. She extended her hand over the arm of the chair and he took it in his.

"When I telephoned, there was only an engaged line signal. I tried several times but I couldn't get through. It seemed best that I come here to make sure all of you were unharmed. Did something happen here?"

"You could say that." Rose filled him in, from veggie-circled plates to the organ recital in Aura Lee's room.

"And don't forget what happened earlier," Aura Lee said.

Rose stared at her blankly.

"You know, the broken mirror in Cottie's room."

Rose sagged. "You know, I'd flat out forgotten it. Goes to show how things have been around here."

"Cottie's mirror broke?" Kerry was crestfallen. "The oval one on the wall?"

"It fell off while we were in her room." Rose sighed. "It was odd, what with Strudel barking madly at it before it fell."

"Don't forget the blood," Aura Lee reminded her.

Noreen glanced at the tiny Band-Aid on Rose's hand. "You cut yourself?"

Rose nodded. "Picking up pieces. It's not serious."

"Tell them about the rug. Oh, and the box," Aura Lee directed.

"Okay, okay." Rose looked down at her hand. "A small box was attached to the mirror and there was a key in it, as well as a circle scratched inside it. Yes, I'll tell them," she said in answer to Aura Lee's sputters. "My blood fell onto the rug in another circle.

That turned black. Okay?" she said flatly with an impatient glance at Aura Lee.

"A perfectly round black circle," Aura Lee emphasized.

"Well." Max pulled at his lower lip as he thought. "That's quite a list," he said finally. "We have several possibilities here. Unless I'm mistaken, you've had a spirit or spirits trying to direct you to several pieces of information." He shook his head. "I must say that what you've described is the most...exciting combination of actions I've ever heard of. If your spirit visitor or visitors have that kind of strength—to knock down a mirror, and to make an organ sound—then we are talking about a significant chain of events."

Aura Lee straightened in her seat, pride filling her face. "It has been quite exciting."

"You mean it's been quite terrifying." Rose turned to Max. "I don't really care about advancing the cause of paranormal research," she said. "I am concerned about living here in fear. We don't know what to expect or when to expect it. Focus, Max, on helping us get to the causes in order to end these events."

Max let out a long breath. "I apologize. It's difficult to hear your experiences without going mental over the amazing aspects of what you've described. I've never encountered anything like it."

"You're lucky." Andrea poured more brandy into her glass. "I've had to confront not only the *idea* of a haunting but of being possessed and directed by one of those spirits doing the haunting. I was lucky not to go completely mental myself."

"Message received." Max rubbed his hands together. "I'd like to suggest that I move in here while the activity is at its height. If I'm here to observe *in situ,* as it were, we might expedite events."

Kerry grinned at him. "You know, you're still talking three-piece suit language."

He raised one brow. "I am British and very well-educated. You'll have to accept me as I am."

"Believe it or not," Kerry said softly, "I don't find that prospect daunting."

"You're both cute as bugs," Brenna said, "but I'm so tired I can't stand it. Tomorrow," she told Max, "I'll tell you about *my* experiences since I arrived, but for now I'm going to bed."

"Sounds like a plan." Rose gathered glasses and headed for the kitchen. "I'm at the point where I defy the spirits to keep me awake. It's been quite a day."

Aura Lee stood up and folded the throw, laying it over the sofa arm. Noreen gathered more glasses and followed Rose into the kitchen.

"Welcome aboard," Andrea said. She rubbed her eyes and yawned. "Where will you stay, at Kerry's or here in the house?"

Max slanted a look Kerry's way. "I rather thought I might beg a night's sleep on your sofa. If that's all right with you."

Kerry was flustered. "Well, of course you're welcome. I think I have clean sheets for it; we can see when we get there."

Max smiled at her. "I'm sure we'll make do." He cupped her elbow and steered her out of the room. "Shall we?"

Brenna watched them leave and turned back toward the kitchen. Her eyes met Andrea's gaze. "And off they go. I imagine extra sheets won't be an issue by the time they get there."

Andrea widened her eyes. "Why, Brenna, whatever do you mean?"

"My heart's going pitter-pat just being near them." Brenna set the decanters back where they belonged and gathered more plates. "I'm glad for Kerry."

"Me, too." Andrea followed her into the kitchen. When she saw Aura Lee bustling between the counter and the dishwasher, she hurried over to her. "Let me do this," she said. "You're out on your feet. It'll only take a little while to clean up. You'll help, won't you?" she asked Brenna.

"Glad to."

"Same goes for you," Andrea told Rose. "Go to bed."

Rose smiled wanly. "You talked me into it. Don't feel you have to make it spotless. If you just load what you can fit in, we'll deal with everything else tomorrow."

"It's a deal. Now go get some sleep."

As she went up the back stairs, Rose felt every day of her fifty-eight years. Too tired to think anymore, she plodded down the hall toward her room. Only the thought of slipping into her bed kept her going. As she reached her door, Rose heard a high-pitched buzzing. She looked around for a bee or wasp that might have become trapped in the house. The sound grew louder as she neared the attic staircase. She recalled the dreadful shrieking from Aura Lee's room, and what she'd said tonight about its beginning with a hum.

Rose moved slowly and quietly, her heart pounding. As she approached the end of the hallway, the overhead light fixture began to glow more brightly.

Now apprehensive on several fronts, Rose edged to the side of the hall in case the glass cover on the fixture exploded. A beam of light shot toward the attic stairs.

Light reflected off a piece of metal on the side of a stair step. Rose caught her breath. She'd seen them a million times, but had never really noticed them. Her gaze climbed from the bottom step to the last near the ceiling. The end of each stair step had been decorated with a small metal disk. The light from the overhead fixture shone on the fifth step from the top. As she drew closer, she could see the tiny opening at the middle of the brass circle. A keyhole.

Rose's mind flashed to the tiny key in her pocket. "I don't believe it." Her eyes widened in surprise. She could see her breath—white vapor—as if she'd exhaled into winter air.

It was frigid in the hall now. Possibilities stuttered through her mind: a window might be open. The wind raging through the trees could have lowered the temperature. The furnace might have gone on the fritz. She crossed her arms over her chest for warmth, her gaze darting about the hallway in search of something to explain why her teeth were chattering.

The glow from the overhead fixture flashed again, then blinked off and on like a strobe light. The drop in temperature was incredible, the chill sinking into her bones. She had to get out of the freezing air. She forced her left leg back, then her right. The sole of one shoe brushed against the runner, nearly tripping her. She stumbled, catching herself against the wall, and regained her footing.

Rose slowly retreated, the unearthly cold lessening as she moved further down the hallway. Her gasps were rapidly building into sobs as she neared the staircase to the kitchen. She groped behind her for the rail. Clutching it with all of her waning strength, she turned around and staggered down the steps.

Andrea looked up from the sink at the sound of footfalls. Astonishment spread across her face as she took in Rose's distress. "What's the matter?" She rushed over to her, the dishtowel forgotten in one hand. Brenna was right behind her.

Rose was dimly aware that she wouldn't be able to go much farther. She dropped unexpectedly onto the bottom step, and swayed forward, letting her head fall to her knees.

Andrea knelt in front of her. She patted Rose's arms and shoulders, trying to figure out what was wrong. "What is it? What's the matter?"

The door next to the stairs opened, and Aura Lee peered around its edge. Her brass-colored hair bristled with several fat rollers. One hand anchored her unbuttoned yellow robe at her neck. "What's going on?" she asked in a wavering voice.

Brenna turned a frightened face to her. "Something's wrong. Rose just came downstairs, and she's in terrible shape."

Aura Lee surged out of her room. "Here, let's get her to a chair." She grabbed Rose's arm, and with Andrea's help hoisted her to her feet. "Come on, now. Just over here."

They walked her to the table, Brenna tailing behind them, and settled her onto the nearest chair. "Is it your heart?" Aura Lee demanded. "Are you having a stroke?"

"No," Rose rasped. "Not physical."

Aura Lee searched her face, then turned away, meeting Andrea's questioning gaze with a shake of her head. "I'll make some tea," she muttered. Bustling to the sink, she snatched the kettle from the stove along the way. She turned on the water, and as her gaze was still fixed on Rose, it spilled over her hand. Exclaiming, she adjusted the flow, then slammed the kettle onto the burner.

"Maybe brandy's a better idea." Brenna took a step toward the dining room, but Rose seized her by the wrist.

"Go upstairs." Her teeth were chattering, and her

hand tightened convulsively, causing Brenna to wince. "Check the light."

Brenna blinked at the fear in Rose's eyes. "Okay." She cast a questioning glance at Aura Lee, who shrugged helplessly. She started to move away, but Rose squeezed her arm even more tightly.

"Andrea, too." Rose's voice shook pitifully. "Don't go alone. Check the stairs to the attic."

Andrea studied her with wide eyes. "You're scaring me, Rose. What's going on?"

"Please." Rose knew she sounded crazy, but she was frantic to know if they would encounter the same circumstances. If the hallway was still so cold, if the light was erratic, she could be sure that what she'd felt was real. Something soft settled on her shoulders and she jerked round to see what it was. Aura Lee had brought a throw from the living room and was tucking it around her. Rose clutched it to her, trying to nod her thanks.

"Come with me," Andrea said to Brenna. "We've got to check out the second floor." Together they headed up the stairs.

"You poor thing." Aura Lee set a cup of tea in front of her. "You drink that now, it'll warm you right up."

Rose wrapped her hands around the cup gratefully. The warmth set off another shudder, and she tried to control it so she could drink the hot liquid. Before she could begin to take a sip, Andrea and Brenna clambered down the steps and came back into the kitchen.

"Well?" Rose examined their faces for reaction.

"It's cold as a mausoleum," Brenna said, "but the light seems okay." She sat in the chair next to her. "What were we supposed to see?"

Rose looked to Andrea, who was pulling out a chair on the other side of the table. "I didn't see anything unusual. Like she said, it was just really cold."

"What's got you so spooked?" asked Brenna.

"The overhead light kept flashing off and on. I thought it might burst. But it wasn't what I saw; it was how I felt. I've never been so cold before." Rose sipped at the tea, and almost spat it out. "Too sweet."

"For shock. Drink it." Aura Lee sounded adamant, but her face was soft with uncertainty. "Did you see her, Rose?"

Rose shook her head. "It was just that god-awful chill. And the light shining on those circles—"

"What?" Aura Lee squeaked.

Rose shivered under the throw, and took another drink of the hot tea. "The light was pointed at the attic stairs. Almost like a spotlight. The decoration on the steps—the ends of them, I mean—are little brass disks. They've probably been there forever." She pulled the throw more firmly around her shoulders. "I don't remember if I ever noticed them. Anyway, one of them has a keyhole in it. And I think it's small enough for the key I found in Caldicott's room."

The sensation caused by that statement took a while to ebb. When it did, Brenna was ready to rush back upstairs immediately.

Rose quailed at the idea. "I can't tell you how terrifying it was. That cold...the feeling that something was waiting." She was already wondering she'd be able to force herself back to her room that night.

"You can't mean for us to wait until morning," Andrea stated in determination. "It's inhuman to ask it of anybody. And you know damn well that Kerry and Noreen will want to see whatever's up there."

Aura Lee glanced uneasily toward the stairs. "I think we ought to wait."

"No way. We can call Noreen, and Kerry and Max

can see whatever we find tomorrow." Andrea's voice was pleading, but impatience flared in her eyes. "Rose, come on! It might not be there in the morning. We don't know what we're dealing with."

"All right. All right." Rose sagged in the chair. "Call Noreen and we'll go check it out together."

Noreen showed up ten minutes after Andrea's call. Sleepy but game, hair spiky, she was warm in a fuzzy green jogging suit. "So, tell me again what's going on?" She yawned mightily.

"I guess we'll find out," Rose answered grimly. She threw off the blanket around her shoulders and got out of the chair.

They went up the back stairs in a cluster thanks to Rose's obvious fear. The air on the second floor was still cold, but that appeared to be the only departure from the ordinary. The overhead lights in the hallway shone without flickering; nothing jumped out at them from the shadowed corners.

By the time they reached the attic stairway, Rose had begun to feel foolish.

"Look. There it is." Brenna pointed at the fifth step. "The key hole is tiny. No wonder no one's ever found it."

They stepped back to allow Rose access to the lock. She was obscurely pleased to see that her hand was steady as she slipped the tiny key into the keyhole. When she turned it, they heard the muffled click of a latch shifting. The end piece of the step moved and a crack appeared. Rose used her fingers to pull the wood piece open all the way.

"What if there are spiders in there?"

Rose hesitated, hand outstretched. "Gee, thanks, Brenna." She forced herself to reach inside the compartment.

"Sorry," Brenna murmured.

"What is it?" Andrea's eyes were fixed on the aperture.

Inside the cubbyhole was a book. Rose pulled it out into the light, and Aura Lee exclaimed, "It's just like the ones Caldicott wrote her journals in."

Rose's lips twisted in the best smile she could muster as she held opened the volume. "Kerry's been hunting for months. I hope this has at least some of what she's been looking for."

She flipped open the book to the middle pages and gazed down at it. "It's written in Caldicott's hand."

Aura Lee gulped back a sob. "I want to know what's in there."

"Me, too." Noreen was pale with fatigue. "But I think we ought to wait until Kerry's here. It wouldn't be right to cheat her out of the discovery."

"All right." Rose closed the book. "But all of you have to see me to my room. If I encounter any other specters tonight, I'll lose my mind."

"You?" Andrea murmured. "Never."

They waited at the door until Rose had checked the closet and looked under the bed. She looked embarrassed, but she made a thorough search. Finally she said, "All right, everything looks okay. Thanks for staying with me."

"No problem," Brenna said.

"Any time." Andrea yawned. "Now let's all get some sleep."

Rose listened to them talking as they went down the back stairs. She took off her clothes and put on her pajamas. As she crawled under the covers, the only thing she could think of was how much she wanted to lie down and lose herself in sleep.

Much to her surprise, she did.

CHAPTER 17

Kerry smoothed the burgundy duvet on the guest room bed and straightened the pillows again. The questions in her mind had her stomach doing somersaults. How was it that Caldicott had never breathed a word about the paranormal to her, but had contacted Max to look into the issue at Wisdom Court? Had her natural skepticism been evident, preventing that disclosure? Was that why Caldicott hadn't given her the information she needed to finish the biography? She paused for a distracted peek at the towels in the adjoining bathroom and finally went back downstairs.

Max was sitting on the sofa, the glass of wine she'd given him in hand. He finished it as she sat down beside him and flicked a look at her under slanted brows. "I thought you'd climbed out a window."

She rolled her eyes in an oh-brother look. "Just checking the accommodations."

"You could have built a bed in the time you were upstairs." The irritation in his voice was unmistakable. "Have you changed your mind about my staying here?" He set the glass back on the coffee table with undue care. As Kerry started to answer, he pressed his lips together, clearly expecting her to ask him to leave.

It was late and Kerry was tired of the undercurrents in their conversations. She leaned against the sofa back, trying to relax. "There's no problem with your staying. I took so long because I was thinking about what you told us earlier, wondering if I screwed up things with Caldicott because I've always thought the paranormal was a bunch of crap."

He shifted his weight, moving closer to her. "Did she ever try to talk to you about it?"

Kerry shook her head. "That's why I was so surprised to hear she'd gotten in touch with you and your association of English ghost-hunters."

Annoyance narrowed his blue eyes. "The Royal Paranormal Society."

"Whatever. I've never had any patience for that stuff, maybe because of how I grew up." He searched her face, waiting. "On a commune in California. Every half-baked notion ever known was embraced and followed until the next one came along." Her glass was nearly empty. "I'll get more wine." She got up and headed for the kitchen, coming back with the bottle of Shiraz and a bag of potato chips. She filled his glass and her own and set the bag between them. "Provisions."

"So you were the child of flower children?" Max stared at her with curiosity.

"I guess you could call them that. Seems overly poetic to me." Kerry was swept with the combination of impatience and *otherness* that always accompanied thoughts of her childhood. "We had to work like dogs just to keep food on the table, but I found time to read and follow my nose as far as education was concerned. I keep in touch with a few of my 'siblings.'"

"And your parents?" Max asked carefully.

Kerry took a drink of wine and tried to keep her cynicism leashed. "Patriarchal traditions were ridiculed, so the kids supposedly belonged to everybody, which meant we didn't belong to anybody. Most of the 'grownups' were heavily into pot, so we pretty much raised ourselves."

"But surely the authorities—"

"—were understaffed and easily bamboozled." Kerry viewed his horror with amusement. "Some of the older kids were actually very good parents. They made sure we younger ones made it to school and kept our noses clean. Then, as we got older, they left to start their own lives and we took over. Most of us did okay. A few ended up serious pot-heads, but they had a good set-up for that and, as far as I know, are happy hanging out at the old digs." She polished off her wine and reached for more. "Needless to say, I don't go home for Christmas."

She hated the expression on his face, the combined outrage and pity she'd seen every time she'd been truthful about her upbringing. "I worked my way through the undergrad years of college," she added hurriedly, "got a fellowship for my masters, and I'm still working on my Ph.D. Caldicott heard me present a paper on similarities in familial units and decided I should write her biography."

"And then she didn't give you what you needed to write it."

Because of the sympathy in his eyes, Kerry just nodded.

"How much more time do you have here?" he asked.

"A little over three months." Kerry fought the panic that rose in her every time she acknowledged how little time was left. "That's nudged me to at least listen to the idea of paranormal influences here. And what happened with Andrea, of course."

Max eyed her in speculation. "You hadn't noticed any odd things happening here? No strange sounds or cold spots?"

"No, not until Andrea showed up." Kerry ate a couple of chips and washed them down with wine. "Even then I didn't experience much of anything. Until we figured out who was behind what she was going through, the trances and her sketches and painting. I saw enough then to convince me that something weird was going on. And there's no way I can deny what happened tonight. Rose told you about the food being moved around, and Aura Lee's organ was played by something no one could see. It counts as paranormal to me."

Max reached for his glass, moving even closer. "The things Ms. Wyntham described to me weren't as dramatic, but she'd accumulated an impressive list of odd events by the time she contacted me. She heard strange sounds on various occasions, particularly a deep growling. The dates she listed were the same as those of pagan ritual days."

Kerry hunched her shoulders against the chill down her spine. "That's creepy."

Max nodded. "Her sleep patterns were affected as well. Tomorrow I'll show you some of the dreams she described." His jaw had tensed and Kerry had the feeling she wouldn't enjoy reading those descriptions.

"Have you encountered things like this before, Max?" The gut-punch of having the lights go out at dinner, of seeing their dinner arranged in patterns was back, fresh in her mind. She rubbed her hands on her slacks and tried to ignore the tremble in them.

"I've seen oddities, and I've felt presences, but it's

the number of signs and manifestations that intrigues me about Wisdom Court." His voice was edgy, and when he took a short breath and let it out, Kerry realized how excited he was.

"I wish I could see it as you do." Part of her was angry at his ability to remain objective, but what she envied was his lack of fear. "We're all so anxious now, waiting for the next surprise." She half-laughed and bent forward for her glass. "It's hell on the nerves."

"I understand."

Kerry turned to meet his eyes. "Why did it take you so long to get here? I mean, Caldicott was expecting you months ago, wasn't she?"

"I was in a car accident." Max looked down at his leg. "You've seen me limp. I was in hospital for a month after it happened, and out of my head during most of that. By the time I got back to normal, Ms. Wyntham was dead." His voice deepened with feeling. "I can't tell you how much I regret that."

Kerry swallowed at the lump in her throat. "She never said a word about any of it to me." She looked blindly at the coffee table. "Why wouldn't she trust me? Why did she close me out of all of it?"

Max slid the rest of the way across the cushion and put his arm around her. "We'll get to the heart of it, luv." She dropped her head to his shoulder and he pulled her firmly against him. "She didn't tell me everything, that I do know, and she made it clear that what she said was confidential."

Kerry savored the strength of his arm around her shoulders. And he was warm. She felt as though she'd been cold forever. "What about the woman she wanted you to trace?"

"Clara Trinder." Max's voice rumbled under her ear. "In her view, Clara Trinder was linked to Wisdom

Court, though she didn't say how. She said something had been set into motion here." His arm tightened. "Looking back, I believe she knew a good deal more than she shared with me."

Kerry sniffed and took the handkerchief he gave her and wiped her eyes. "But why—how did she come to contact you?"

Max smiled down at her. "My dear girl, I'm one of the top men in the paranormal world. Of course she came to me."

"Humble, aren't you?" Kerry felt comfortable with him, and wondered why they'd been so snarky to each other. When she glanced up at him and saw his frown, some of her ease faded and she pulled back. Max firmly returned her against his side and bent to kiss her.

His lips were warm and moved enticingly against hers. She put her arms around him and he deepened the kiss. His tongue stole into her mouth and at the taste of him she felt a surge of desire. "Max," she murmured against his mouth as he ran one hand down her back and up again.

She stroked his hair, fingers taking pleasure in the smooth strands, and when she moved against him he tightened his hold on her.

Max lifted his head and Kerry was entranced by the thickness of his lashes, by the intense expression in his eyes. "I thought you couldn't stand me."

He ran his hand down her back again, setting off ripples of pleasure along her spine. "You've got a mouth on you. I wanted to kiss it to shut you up."

"Just try it," she said in a prim voice. "See what it gets you." As his arms tightened around her, she lifted her head and leaned in. His lips caught hers, rubbed against her, side to side and desire shivered through her.

"Let's go upstairs." Had she said it or had he? She didn't know, didn't care.

He stood up and held out one hand. When she put hers in it, he pulled her to her feet. His blue eyes focused on her and she couldn't help but smile.

"Something amusing?" he asked.

"You." Her smile grew and she felt a swell of emotion. "You are a lovely man."

His fingers tightened on hers. "If you're delusional enough to believe that, luv, I need to get you into bed before the spell wears off." He tugged her toward the stairs and she followed.

They were near the top step when Max stopped. His breath sucked in sharply and his hand tightened on hers.

"What is it?" She heard the quaver in her voice and felt a spurt of anger.

"Don't you feel the cold?" Max turned his head and looked down at her.

His expression scared her. She shook her head. Suddenly he pulled her up the last two steps through frigid air that made her stumble.

"Come on. *Move*." He dragged her the short distance to her room and pulled her through, slamming the door behind them. His arms came around her and he held her so tightly she couldn't take a full breath.

"What was that?" she whispered.

"I don't know," he breathed.

Brenna was near the front door when she heard a noise behind her. She spun around, nearly colliding with Andrea, who took a quick step back, both hands lifted defensively. "Sorry, sorry. Didn't mean to scare you."

Brenna sagged in relief. "You never know what's

behind you around here."

"No kidding." Andrea pointed at the stack of envelopes and magazines on the table by the stairs. "I was just checking for mail."

Brenna's glance ricocheted off the pile. "Any chance you'd walk me to my place? I'm kind of freaking out. The quiet around here is getting to me."

"Spooked, huh?" Andrea's voice was sympathetic.

"Yeah." Brenna pulled up her jacket zipper and turned toward the door.

"Sure, I'll walk you." Andrea jerked her coat from the row of hooks and followed her. "Guess I'm too tired to be freaking."

"Lucky you."

Stars studded the sky and the crescent moon hung like a crooked smile over the Flatirons. Brenna shivered in the chill. "I've been all over L.A. at night, but I don't like being alone in the dark after what happened tonight. I thought Rose was going to lose it in there. Maybe have a heart attack."

"I don't blame her." Andrea shoved her hands in her pockets. "I did not want to go up those stairs."

A few dry leaves, stirred by a breeze, whispered across the cobblestone courtyard and Brenna twitched a quick look behind her. "You looked plenty brave when you led the way up."

"Yeah, right." Andrea's lips twisted and the self-disgust in her eyes was heavy enough to thud on the cobblestones. "Like I'm going to tell Rose I don't want to check out the second floor when she looks like Death munching on a cracker." She stopped at the stairs to the associate house. "We're here on the street where you live."

Brenna hunched her shoulders. "Okay, so now I go inside."

"Want me to go in with you?"

"No." Brenna let out a breath. "I'll be fine."

"I didn't think till now, but you're welcome to stay at my place tonight. We could finish off the brownies and wait for ghosts to show up."

"Tempting." Brenna tried to smile. "I'm here. Path of least resistance and all that." She started up the steps and stopped. It was easier to look at Andrea than up the stairs to the door. "Thanks, though. Rain check for the ghosts?"

"No worries. I think we'll all be sharing more of those." Andrea waited for Brenna to unlock the outside door. "See you tomorrow."

"Yeah, see you." Brenna slid inside, pushing the front door shut behind her. She was halfway to her apartment when the overhead lights flickered and died.

"Shit." Her whisper hissed and then rustled through the hall, echoing from every direction.

So this is pitch black. Brenna turned her head back and forth, unable to find even a sliver of light. The main door was behind her. Her door ought to be on the left. She took a step and was hit with a feeling of total isolation. *No light, no warmth, no anchor.* She took another step and reached with both hands, keys dangling from the right, jingling together as she moved. The tinny vibrations stretched like a beast freed from a cage, building into an ear-splitting clanging. She waved her arms, frantic to find the wall, but felt nothing. *It's a hallway! I can cross it in a few steps.*

Deciding she was pointed in the right direction, she walked straight ahead: one, two, three steps, and collided with a wall. The keys slipped from her hand and jangled as they landed. *On the tile by the carpet runner.* Brenna bent down through the harsh ringing pounding against her ears.

"What the hell." The words bounced shouting back at her, echoing, speeding up. She slapped along the edge of the runner and finally brushed against the keys and grabbed them.

Brenna threw out one hand, barely noticing the pain when it struck plaster. She shoved the keys into her pocket and started hitting the wall with both hands. She scooted along the baseboard, the dull thuds of her search resounding from all directions, building in volume.

Like an echo chamber, have to get out of here. Ears ringing, heart beating double time, Brenna kept moving, hands feeling desperately for the door.

When she encountered vertical molding, she groped upward, finally banging her knuckles against the doorknob. She pulled herself up and reached into her pocket for the keys. Finding the lock, she felt for the keyhole and tried to slide in the key. *Has to be my door.* Her hands were shaking and the small, scratchy noises of metal against metal were amplified, beating against her ears.

"Stop it, stop it," she muttered. The tip of the key slid into the slot, but when she tried to turn it, nothing happened.

Other key. She fumbled to get a firm hold on the second key. After struggling to match the pieces of metal, the key slipped into the lock and turned.

Brenna shouldered her way in, almost falling into the room. She spun to shove the door shut behind her, turning the bolt immediately as she flailed for the light switch. The lamp on the foyer table flared like a searchlight and she shut her eyes against it.

After a moment Brenna opened them and turned to look around, going far enough inside to peer into the living room. Everything appeared to be undisturbed. She took a faltering step back toward the door, then another. Placing her ear against the wood, she listened. Nothing. A glance through the peephole showed the lighted hallway.

Brenna rested her forehead against the oak door. Her first thought was to call Rose and everyone else for reinforcement. *What could they do?* Stiffening her resolve, she listened again, ear pushed against the wood. With reluctance she turned the bolt and opened the door a crack, straining to hear any sound. After a moment she widened the gap to stick her head out.

The hall, scented as always with lemons and beeswax, was silent.

Brenna closed the door carefully and locked it before she sank to the floor. Relief swept through her as she huddled, arms around her knees. *What was it, what could have caused those sounds? What kind of lunacy is going on here?*

She dug in her coat pocket for a tissue, fingers brushing against her cell phone. She speed-dialed Dink before she could think about it. When she heard his voice she lost what little control she had left. "Dink—oh, God, Dink." Choppy sobs overtook her.

"Bren? What the hell—" Dink's voice was harsh. "Are you okay? What's going on?" When she didn't answer, just continued crying, he said with force, "Brenna! Tell me what's happening. Are you all right?"

She took a deep breath, then another. "Sorry," she gulped. "Sorry."

"Don't be sorry. Tell me what it is."

"Okay." She pushed herself up off the floor. "Let me get a Kleenex." She wobbled into the living room, the last of the sobs dying out, and found the tissue box. When she'd blown her nose, taken a deep breath, she said, "Okay, I'm sorry I lost it."

Dink swore in her ear. "For chrissake, Bren—"

"Oh, Dink, I'm so scared. Wisdom Court is haunted—"

"*What?*" Brenna pulled the phone away from her ear, and replaced it when he quieted.

"It's haunted here. I'm not kidding. I was just trapped in the entrance hall with something—I don't know what—and the lights went out, and the sound— God, the sound, Dink, like a giant reverb chamber, and I couldn't see. I'm so damned scared I don't know what to do." She was crying and couldn't stop.

"Brenna," he said helplessly. "Babe, settle down, I can't understand what you're saying. Talk to me, you're killing me here."

"Dink," she whispered, "something scary crazy is going on here and it's getting worse."

NIGHTMIRROR

Missing chessmen, empty board
No someone here, just a void
Tot up the squares, search for the rows
Gone.

Loose ends, crumbs, the grains of who
Slide off the landscape, decline to nil
The wind yawns, bored, and scatters scraps.
Gone.

Please, please don't go
Please, please come back

Empty station, no travelers found
A house deserted, echoes sound
Dust in the corners, tissue on the floor
Gone.

Fear at the door, peeks through the crack.
Smiles. You're next
Gone.

CHAPTER 18

Brenna forced her eyes open, relieved when she saw her bedroom instead of the frozen chessboard of her dream. *God. That was a bad one.*

She pushed the bedcovers aside and swung her legs over the edge of the mattress, shivering in the chilly air. Her hoodie was at the foot of the bed and she slid her arms into the sleeves, hugging the warm material to her body. She'd thought she was over the nightmares. She'd been in Boulder six days and she'd had one nearly every night. How long would she have to live with them?

She headed for the bathroom and began her morning drill, including the familiar pep talk. The faucet handle twisted under her hand as she reminded herself of what the hospice counselors had told her, that grief would come and go at its own pace. Healing had no timetable. She needed to acknowledge her feelings rather than fight them. If she relied on her support group all would be well.

Her support group was Dink and he was in L.A. "So I dream," she muttered. And those dreams were kicking her emotional ass. Brenna let the hot shower spray over her head and down her back, visualizing shards of the nightmare flowing down the drain.

When she stepped out of the shower, her shoulders were relaxed and her head was clear. Enfolding her hair in a towel, she grabbed another to wrap around her body. Brenna was squeezing lotion into one hand when she glanced at herself in the mirror. The bottle slid from her fingers to the floor.

On the foggy surface of the glass was scrawled an uneven five-pointed star.

Her breath hitched and her head began to spin. The strength leached from her knees and she sank onto the bathroom floor. Her head fell to her chest and she wept.

The sun pouring through the big window highlighted the shadows under Brenna's eyes. Andrea held her breath as Brenna poured coffee and sighed in relief when the shaking carafe was returned to the machine without spilling all over the counter. "What do *you* think the stars mean?"

"I don't know." Brenna clutched her cup, bringing it to her lips cautiously, barely sipping from it. "None of them make any sense. First I thought somebody was messing with my film, but when I took it to the guy at the processing place, the stars were gone. He thinks I'm crazy." She flicked a cynical look at Andrea. "I don't know what to think about the one on the mirror." She set down the cup. "Either somebody real came in and drew it when I was in the shower, which is creepy as hell, or…" Her bottom lip quivered. "Or something I can't see was able to draw it, which is beyond scary." She swallowed and pushed out a few more words. "I don't like either option."

"Aura Lee would say something's trying to communicate with you," Andrea said softly.

"Jesus, that's no comfort." Brenna rubbed at the base of her skull.

Andrea gasped at the purple mark on her skin. "What happened to your hand? That's a hell of a bruise on the edge."

Brenna didn't look at it. "I banged it against the wall last night."

"What? Climbing it?"

"As good as. After you walked me home, something happened." She hunched her shoulders at Andrea's raised brows. "I came inside and everything looked okay. Then the lights in the hall went out."

"Brenna!"

Brenna nodded. "It was pitch dark. I couldn't see anything, but the real freak-out was the sound. Every tiny bit was amplified. It was like the noises were alive and growing. I dropped my keys and the jangle just built, like in an echo chamber. Pretty soon it was blasting my ears and I couldn't think."

"I'll bet," muttered Andrea.

"I swore or something and the words echoed, first in whispers, then building into screaming. I was feeling around for the keys like a maniac, and that's when my hand hit the wall. I finally found them, and felt my way to the door. I got in here and shook like a fool for a while. When I could stand it, I opened the door. The lights were on. No noise at all."

"You opened the door?" The look Andrea shot her was heavy with respect. "I would've hid under the bed. No kidding," she added at Brenna's weak smile. "No way would I have gotten anywhere near that hallway."

Brenna sagged against the sofa back. "Then I had a truly awful dream, worse than the rest, and they're bad enough. I feel like a mental case, and that's not good right now."

"It isn't good anytime. What kind of dreams?"

"Nasty ones." She rubbed both hands over her face and then looked at Andrea. "About my grandmother—she died last year."

"I'm sorry." Andrea patted Brenna's shoulder. "Were you close?"

"She raised me after my mom left." In answer to the question in Andrea's face, Brenna added, "I was nine."

"That's rough."

"It would've been if it hadn't been for Gran. She was wonderful." Brenna's lips moved in a smile but it didn't reach her eyes. "She worked as a studio makeup artist, started at RKO in the forties, and later went to MGM." She folded her legs under her and leaned against the sofa arm. "Gran really *was* an artist. She could make the most ordinary person look gorgeous. When I was about thirteen..." Brenna's eyes brightened as she remembered. "You want to be pretty more than anything at that age, but you haven't grown into your face yet. I pestered her, though, and she gave in. She stared at me for the longest time. It was getting uncomfortable, but then she reached into her kit and told me to sit back in the chair.

"Gran got out her brushes and started on my eyebrows and cheek bones. I couldn't see what she was doing 'cause she draped a towel over the mirror. She was cracking jokes the whole time she was putting stuff on my face, stupid kid jokes, knock-knocks, that kind of thing." Brenna's laugh broke in the middle. "When she was done she stood looking at me like before. She had an old-fashioned scent bottle. You know, the kind with a bulb. She sprayed me once with her own perfume, Wind Song, and then she tugged the towel off the mirror. When I saw myself, I couldn't believe it."

Her cheeks were pink, her eyes cloudy with memory. "I guess I expected thick makeup, you know? That she was using her equipment to give me a thrill. Instead, she showed me what I'd probably look like when I grew up. She saw the adult me in my kid face and used her makeup to reveal it. It was magical, unforgettable. And she talked about how I was going to make it in Hollywood, that I was a good enough photographer to do it."

Brenna's lips quivered and the anguish in her eyes drew Andrea closer to her. She put her arm around her shoulders. "She had Alzheimer's. By the time she died, she didn't remember my face. For a while she thought I was my mother." She struggled to control her voice. "Gran would call me by her name, Diane. After a few months, she didn't remember who Diane was, and she thought I was her sister or her mother. Then she stopped calling me by any names. She hardly talked, but when she did, she acted like a girl herself. If what she said was true, I learned a lot about what it was like for her."

"Oh, Brenna," murmured Andrea.

"She had a crappy childhood, and she ran off to Hollywood before she was eighteen. All those stories about the dirty old men running the studios? Well, if what Gran said was true, they didn't save their lousy behavior just for actresses. She was a pretty girl, too. I've got a couple of snapshots. I don't know if she ever interviewed on her back, but from a few things she said toward the end, she might have."

Brenna looked down at her hands. "I'll never know for sure." She drew her wrist across her eyes, and it came away wet. "Every piece of her was destroyed. No dignity, no self. By the end, I was praying for her to die. I just wanted it to end for her, and for me."

Andrea rested her head on Brenna's shoulder and

held her more tightly. "Poor girl," she murmured. "Poor girl."

"I feel so guilty," Brenna choked. "She always built me up, told me I had talent, an eye for pictures, that I'd have my own star on the Walk of Fame. *You're gonna be a star, chickie.* She told me that so many times. She was the only family I had and I wanted to kill her to stop her suffering. I couldn't figure out how to do it and still look at myself in the mirror every day. Now I'm scared it's genetic, that I'll end up like her, and that's so selfish and cold." She broke down.

Andrea cradled Brenna against her as she cried. She whispered comfort words, nonsense words, just as she had when her daughter Grace had run to her with a skinned knee or a schoolyard betrayal. "It'll be all right, it'll be all right."

It would never be all right, but Brenna already knew that.

The tears passed and Brenna pulled herself together. She excused herself for a trip to the bathroom and Andrea slumped against the sofa. Life is so unfair, she thought for the millionth time in her life. Closing her eyes, she breathed deeply to deal with the jagged feelings Brenna had loosed.

"Kerry."

She turned toward the sound, eyes closed, drifting on a tide of pleasure. *So happy.* Her nose twitched at the scent of cinnamon.

"Kerry." The voice was thick, rusty, unused for too long.

The warmth held her immobile and she yearned to stay in the soft river of comfort. It was the humming that had her opening her eyes.

In the gray of early morning the small flickering light barely caught her attention. Triangular, it hovered for a long moment and slowly began to move. It slid across the patterned plaster and she thought it a reflection from a car's headlights. *It's just someone going up Flagstaff road.* The light stopped again before it raced across the ceiling and skimmed down the wall.

Kerry blinked sleepily and yawned, turning to snuggle against Max. His eyes were closed and he inhaled and exhaled the slow breaths of deep sleep. She wondered that he'd called her name as he slept, but soon drifted off on the thought.

Kerry's cell phone chimed and she surged to a sitting position, heart pounding. Grabbing it, she flipped it open and croaked, "Hello?" A shaft of sunlight stabbing through the bedroom window blinds forced her eyes shut.

"Kerry, it's Rose." When she didn't respond, she added, "I hope I didn't wake you. It's almost ten."

"Um, no, of course not." She started to push her hair out of her eyes, but Max caught her hand and pulled it to his mouth, kissing her fingers. She looked down at him, feeling a sloppy grin spread across her face.

"Kerry? Are you there?" Max was licking between her fingers with the tip of his tongue, the soft friction of his lips sending shivers up her arm.

Kerry struggled to round up a few brain cells. "Sorry. My mind's wandering. I didn't sleep much." *Because, in between making like Ghostbusters, Max and I were exploring other ways of communicating.*

"Is Max there?"

Kerry tugged her hand out of his grasp. "I think he's on the phone in the other room." She stuck out her tongue at his mischievous smile. "Can I ask him to call you back?"

She heard Aura Lee in the background before Rose

spoke again. "We need to talk to both of you about something that happened last night. Can the two of you come here for brunch? Aura Lee just took cranberry muffins out of the oven."

"Sure. What happened?"

"It's a long story. We'll discuss it when you get here."

Kerry frowned, curious at the flustered note in Rose's voice. "Ten-thirty okay?"

"We'll see you then."

Kerry set down the phone.

"You look worried, luv," Max murmured. "Is anything wrong?"

"Rose said something happened last night." She gnawed at one thumbnail until he pulled her hand away from her mouth. "Considering what went on before we left, I wonder what it was."

"*We* happened last night," he stated firmly. "I'm in hopes of our happening again."

"That's one way of putting it." Kerry glanced over her shoulder at the clock and bent to him, finding his mouth with her own. "We have a half hour before we meet up with Rose." She nipped at his lips. "You want a shower or do you want to mess around?"

Max didn't dignify the question with a response. Not a verbal one.

CHAPTER 19

A chilly wind pushed Kerry and Max toward the main house across the cobblestone square. Swaying tree branches creaked in protest as silver clouds tumbled toward Boulder from the northern horizon.

They hurried up the porch steps and slipped inside, slamming it shut, both leaning on it until Kerry made sure the latch had caught. As she turned toward him, flushed and smiling, Max pulled her toward him. To her delight, he kissed the tip of her nose.

"Well, well," quavered Noreen from the arched entry to the dining room. *"The heart swells with attachment like a storm-tossed topgallant sail filled by the force of a storm.* Eliza Justice Belmont..." her voice died away.

Kerry's laugh at the terrible quotation stopped short when she really looked at Noreen. Her face was ashen and she held her arms against her chest as if in the grip of bone-deep cold, despite her thick sweater. "What's wrong?"

"Apparently our unwelcome visitors are active today." Her voice trembled. "No," she added as they began to take off their jackets. "Leave them on. It's cold in the kitchen." Noreen extended her hand to Max. "Come along, the others are anxious to get started."

Concerned, Max took Noreen's hand and walked beside her. Kerry hurried along behind, her heart thumping faster, a feeling of dread sliding over her like a piece of clothing.

The scent of cranberry muffins couldn't combat the air of fatigue and frayed nerves in the group seated at the table. And Noreen was right that it was cold. Andrea was at one end, her jean jacket zipped to her chin, propping up her head with both hands. Brenna hunched on a chair at one side, hood pulled over her hair. Her weary eyes told of interrupted sleep.

Aura Lee was pasty-faced and her scarlet caftan was half-covered by a crocheted shawl. She carried two mugs of coffee to the table. "I'm so glad you're here."

"I'm glad, too." Max pulled out a chair for Kerry and took his place beside her. "What's the situation?"

"None of us can get warm so we've left on the oven." Rose took a book from the counter and brought it to the table. "I don't know if our invisible friends disapprove of our activities last night, or if they can't help casting a chill."

Kerry was shocked at her pallor. "You look terrible. Which activities?"

Rose shook her head. "After you two left last night, we had another *adventure*." Her voice was heavy with sarcasm. She picked up her coffee cup but only took a sip, setting the cup down, touching the book cover.

Kerry leaned toward her. "Something else? Why didn't you—"

Rose held up her hand. "Hold on a minute and I'll tell you." She rested her hands on the book. "When I went up to bed I was directed to something you've been trying to find."

"Directed?" Kerry shook her head in confusion. "What're you talking about?"

"Long story short: thanks to a cold spot from hell and a disco ball effect in the hall, we found the hidey hole you've been looking for. Ironically, it was fairly near where we were looking yesterday."

Kerry felt a jolt of hope that made her heart beat faster. "Are you telling me—"

Rose pushed the book across the table, the lines of worry at the corners of her eyes deepening as Kerry pulled it to her, lifting the cover with care.

She took in a sharp breath and let it out, then read the title aloud. "*My Personal Journal: 1939 to 1945*." Kerry looked up from the page, shaken. "That's what was written on the scrap of paper I found in Max's book." She ran her fingers lightly over the page, feeling only the smooth surface. "Nothing's been torn out." She looked to Max in confusion and pushed the volume toward him. "How could that be?"

Max ran his hands over the paper. "There's not a crease or any other damage." He shot a look at Rose, and Kerry suppressed a shiver at the grim purpose in them. "I want to hear about what happened, all the details."

"You'll get them, but not right now. All of us— especially Kerry—need to know what's in that journal."

"Amen to that." Kerry's chest tightened and she forced herself to take another deep breath. "I hope it tells us more than we know so far." She opened the volume, and began to read.

I write this memoir with reluctance, but I've come to see it is necessary. Things set into motion long ago have grown in power and the ones who remain must know in order to see

*that Wisdom Court survives. My strength is
waning. I must use it to shore up the defenses
I put into place at the beginning.*

Andrea gasped aloud and Noreen looked at her
sharply. "Someone walked across my grave," Andrea
said and trembled again. "Ugh, that's cheerful."

"You're pale as a ghost." Aura Lee looked
dismayed. "I'm sorry, I'm as bad as you are. I mean,
we're both crepe-hangers today." She waved her
hands in the air in frustration. "Never mind."

Rose rolled her eyes and turned to Kerry. "You
want to keep reading?"

Kerry looked down at the page again, fingers
tightening on the journal.

*I have long focused on living in the present,
rarely pausing to look back at what happened
long ago. When one has killed herself, it's
hard to return to the scene of the death, for
fear of experiencing it all again.*

"What's she talking about?" Aura Lee's voice
cracked with distress. "She killed herself? What does
that mean?"

"We'll find out, I think," Rose said. She caught the
concern on Noreen's face and something passed
between them. "We may not like what we learn,"
Rose murmured.

Aura Lee's posture stiffened. "This is Cottie we're
talking about. She was one of the best people ever."
She motioned to Kerry. "Keep going."

*I've been known as Caldicott Wyntham for
many years, but I gave myself that name after
the war. I was born Clara Trinder, the
daughter of Molly Trinder, sometime barmaid.
She didn't talk much about her life before I*

*came along, but I've discovered some things
here and there. When I was a child and asked
questions about my father, she'd laugh and
say she found me under a cabbage leaf. From
the village children I learned I was a bastard,
that Mum was seen as a tart. I learned the
meaning of that term early.*

"Wait." Rose turned to Max. "Isn't that the name of
the woman Cottie hired you to find?"

"Clara Trinder," said Max quietly. "I wasn't told
that she and Ms. Wyntham were the same person."

Brenna frowned. "She hired you to find herself?"
She hunched her shoulders and looked around. "Is it
just me or is it getting colder in here?"

"I feel it, too." Max glanced at the others, brow
raised. "Would you agree?"

Rose was clutching her arms. "It's not just you. I'll
turn up the furnace." She went out of the room and
returned a short time later. "The place ought to feel
like a sauna in a few minutes." She sat down. "Go on,
Kerry."

Kerry resumed reading.

*Mum said I might have been born near the
village of Kettleworth in Northumberland, in
1920. I honestly think she forgot where the
blessed event occurred. She said my birth was
never recorded, so God knows the
circumstances. I never knew my grandparents
on either side and Mum didn't tell me who
they were. I've always thought they cast her
out, giving me no reason to concern myself
with any of them.*

*Mum worked as a barmaid in many of the
pubs in the many villages we came to, but she
wanted me to be more. I was sent to school*

wherever we lived, and she always asked the local vicar to give me a list of books to read in order to improve myself. I never attended the schools for long because we always left before we set down roots. "Something new is around the corner," Mum would say, and soon we'd be on our way.

We moved from Cheltenham to Birmingham a year before she died. By then she'd invented a dead father for me—a vicar's assistant at that—and set out to establish me with a proper job or a suitable husband. Looking back, I believe she knew she was dying, and was anxious to see me cared for. I'm glad she never knew what a price I paid for trying to move up in the world. She was a true democrat, my Mum, ahead of her time.

She breathed her last in a hospital charity ward. I stayed at her bedside holding her hand, so thin, so still. The edge of the blue counterpane covering her was frayed. I was frightened by the way she looked at me, with pity in her eyes. "I'm sorry, luv," she said, and I didn't know what she meant. I was eighteen, yet didn't understand she was going to leave me that day. "Do your best, luv," she murmured. "It'll get you somewhere." And she died. I held her hand until it was cold. She was the only person in the world who loved me.

Aura Lee wiped her cheeks with a crumpled tissue. "That sweet girl, left all alone at such an early age."

Rose swallowed and pressed her lips together for a moment. "The world was in a hell of a mess. The Depression and England on the edge of war. She's already hinted she had a rough time. Can we handle whatever we find out about her?"

"She was my friend and yours," said Aura Lee. "If we can't accept who she was, then who can?"

"Did you find anything with the book?" Kerry drank the rest of her coffee and set down her cup. "I'm wondering when she wrote this. Clearly it wasn't a diary she kept at the time these things happened."

"There wasn't anything else," Rose said. "It was inside one of the stair steps to the attic. After we read it, I'll check the other steps to see if more is hidden. Maybe all the other stairs as well." Her shoulders sagged as she let out a long breath. "I don't understand the secrecy. Why would she go to such lengths to hide her journal in such a place?"

"Maybe she tells us in the journal." Max touched Kerry's cheek. "Will you continue or do you want one of us to help?"

Kerry leaned against his palm for a moment. "I'll keep going for now." She smiled at the others. "I've waited so long for this."

Andrea nodded and Brenna returned her smile.

After Mum died, I was lost. The vicar found light cleaning and childcare jobs to keep me busy, but I recall very little of the work or the people involved. I kept going, as I knew Mum would want me to do.

One day realized I had need of real work and a plan.

Everywhere I looked was something to make me think of Mum. I decided to leave Birmingham to get away from the reminders. I thought perhaps London would be the place, but the housekeeper at St. Aidan's took a hand in my future.

She befriended me during Mum's final illness. Her sister was leaving her job as a clerk to the vicar of a small parish in Buckinghamshire. She wrote her sister about me, and her sister pressed my case with the vicar. Before long I was on my way to take her place with a promise of two pounds/six shillings per week and a place to live.

It was remarkably easy. The vicar and his wife introduced me to a young woman needing someone to share her bed-sitting room. I'll call her Flo, a farmer's daughter saving her money to go to London to find a husband. "Looking after a man is better than looking after a herd of cows," she said, and practiced on the young men of the parish, who were responsive to her chestnut curls and rounded figure.

During the day I worked in the tiny church office, typing up committee minutes, making copies of Sunday bulletins on the duplicator. Evenings I read books and plotted which museums I'd see when I ventured to London on my first holiday. Trying to improve myself was a habit, thanks to Mum. Flo had little patience with it.

"Soon all the dishy men will be off fighting the Germans," she told me. "There's a dance at the Hall and it's our duty to dance with them." Who was I to shirk my duty?

The next two years were filled with dancing and picnics with young men soon to be at war. We worked harder than ever at our jobs and lived for such moments of gaiety as we could find.

And that is how I came to meet Duncan, he of the haunted brown eyes and a face carved in strong, beautiful lines. He had thick black hair, a whippet lean body, and a rare smile. I was swept away at our first meeting at a small country-dance, as was he. After all this time, I dare not mention his real name or the estate where he was born. It is still too dangerous.

"What in the world does she mean by that?" Noreen exclaimed, breaking the spell of the narrative.

Brenna took the opportunity to uncoil her legs and stand up. Kerry set down the book and slid out of her chair to head for the bathroom. Max stood, stretching his arms over his head. "The woman could write," he said.

"Yes, she could. I feel as though I've been there with her." Rose glanced at the cups on the table and got up to top off a few. "I imagine Kerry could use some water."

Aura Lee said nothing. Her face had settled into lines of sorrow, her body slumped in the chair.

Rose paused beside her. "What is it?"

"She never said a word about any of it." Aura Lee's lips twisted. "We were friends, or so I thought, but there was never a word about any of this."

"Maybe she couldn't stand to talk about it." Noreen pushed herself out of her chair and surveyed Aura Lee with sympathetic eyes. "Think of the gap between where she starts this story, just a girl in a world on the edge of war, and her ending up here at Wisdom Court. I can't imagine what she went through to make the transition. We all have past experiences we don't talk about, don't we?"

Aura Lee's nod was rueful. "You're right about that." She reached for Noreen's hand and squeezed it.

Kerry came back and Noreen said, "My turn," and left the kitchen.

"It's still cold." Max looked about the room in curiosity. "Have there been any other differences this morning? Items out of place," he said to Rose's quizzical expression. "More of the circles you described yesterday?"

Rose frowned, considering. "No," she said, "nothing I can think of at the moment. Did you notice anything?" she asked Aura Lee.

"Just the cold." Then her eyes widened. "Wait, Strudel was acting oddly at first. When we came in here she ran over to the corner." She pointed to the area beside the window near Brenna. "She was wagging her tail like she does when she sees someone she likes…" Her eyes filled with tears. "Do you think she could have sensed Cottie?" Her gaze flew back to the corner. "Cottie?"

Max went around the table to put his hand on her shoulder. "I appreciate how hard this is for you. There's no way to know for certain she's been here."

Kerry cupped her coffee mug in her hands and took a sip. "I guess the temperature variation could suggest that Cottie's listening, but we can't be sure."

"Do you have some paper and a pen?" Max asked Rose. "I should have noted the conditions to create a baseline for comparisons." He glanced at Kerry. "I've been distracted, I'm afraid."

Kerry smiled down at her cup.

Rose nodded and left the table, heading for the dining room. When she returned, her eyes were troubled. "According to the thermostat, it's seventy-nine degrees in the house."

"We'll take that as an indication of a visitor's presence. Will you continue, luv?" he asked Kerry.

CHAPTER 20

From the beginning it was deadly serious between Duncan and me. When our eyes met, each of us was tied to the other. I can describe it in no other way. After a lifetime of never having a place, I belonged to Duncan, and he to me.

Looking back, I recall how the sound of the music simply died away as our steps slowed until we were still. In a bubble of silence Duncan took me by the hand and led me away from the dance floor. We made our way to the shadows at the edge of the room and sat in folding chairs just looking at one another.

He told me he was just down from Oxford to talk to his father about joining the RAF. He knew war was coming and he wanted to do his part. His fingers tightened around mine. "Of course, this complicates things."

I nodded, but for me all had become simple.

Our talk was charged with a connection of another kind. As I told him of Mum's death and how I'd come there, his eyes were fixed on my lips. I could feel his gaze, almost like a touch. I saw the sympathy in his face but I was more intent upon his thick black lashes. With the warmth of his strong hand holding mine came a feeling I'd never known. I was at home. He was my home. But I also realized we had so little time. Soon he would be going to fight, and where would that leave us? Having found each other, would Fate separate us so soon?

Duncan read my mind and smiled. "We've been given a great gift," he said with confidence. "Stop trying to measure it and just accept it. We'll make do, my love, indeed we will." He guided me back to the dance floor and we moved to the music in each other's arms until the band members stopped playing. It was heavenly.

Flo signaled me from the door, where she stood by the side of a tall, thin ensign. I nodded toward Duncan and waved her on. Duncan would take me home and we would see each other the following day. He delivered me to my door and kissed me, holding me in his arms for a long time. I dreamed of him the entire night and awoke the next morning half-convinced it had all been a delusion.

Things began to go wrong almost immediately. When Duncan arrived that morning, he was deeply angry. His father had raged at the idea of his even thinking of entering the military. He was of the persuasion that England would continue to appease Germany, which would achieve its aspirations for expansion and would become the leading country in Europe. How odd now to recognize what an enormous impact the Nazi sympathies of Duncan's father had on my life. Ultimately, they led me to the creation of Wisdom Court. I would take this story to my grave were I not alarmed for the safety of the Wisdom Court residents, past and present.

Kerry looked up from the page. "Get me a blanket, will you?" Her voice shook.

Max was out of his chair in an instant, bending over her in concern. "Your lips are bluish." He looked at the others, frowning at their pale faces and hunched shoulders. "I suggest we go into the living room and light the fire."

Noreen pushed away from the table and stood up stiffly. She held onto the chair back for a moment to steady herself. "Good idea. I'm so cold I can't think of a quote to cite."

"That's definitely serious." Rose helped Aura Lee out of her chair and guided her to the door.

Andrea and Brenna stayed behind. "Let them get the fire going while we put on the kettle." Andrea went to the stove. "Hot chocolate sounds good to me."

Brenna stared at her in wonder. "Vapor is coming from your mouth!" She looked down toward her lips. "Mine, too. Can it be that cold?"

"Evidently. And I thought it was weird last time." Andrea turned off the faucet and slammed the kettle onto the stove. "I hate not knowing what's behind these disturbances!" She turned on the burner. "All I want is to be able to work, to experience my year here and then go to the next thing. Instead we're living in a freaking haunted house." She sounded on the edge of tears.

Brenna was startled at the bitterness in her voice.

"You're really scared, aren't you?"

"Aren't you?" Andrea leaned against the counter. "What I went through when I first got here made me question myself, my very sanity. We worked together to figure out what was causing the haunting." Her hands clenched into fists. "We. Resolved. It. When nothing else happened for a while I came to believe it was all over. I *hate* that the fear has come back." She whirled and started pulling cups out of the cupboard in short, sharp motions.

"Maybe we can resolve it again."

Andrea turned to her. "Brenna, it's worse this time. Look at how many things have happened in just the last couple of days. I believe more spirits are trying to get through to us. And they're stronger, able to manipulate conditions, the temperature and the lights. For the love of God! We're both fogging up the kitchen! We can't live like that. Don't you remember how scared you were last night?"

"What happened last night?" Rose stood in the doorway, and by the look of her, braced for another blow.

Brenna shook her head. "Just one more incident. We can talk about it later."

"No." Andrea took a step toward her. "You have to tell them. It's important." Andrea turned toward Rose. "She's had her own visitation, and it was a doozy."

"All right. Come to the living room. We'll talk about it." Rose caught sight of the kettle on the lit burner. "You're one step ahead of me. I thought warm drinks might revive us a little. Aura Lee said more muffins are in the pantry." She tried to smile. "I think we could all use the carbs."

"Tea and hot chocolate will be ready shortly," Andrea said. "You want to see who wants what?"

"Sure." Rose started out of the room, paused and

looked over her shoulder at Brenna. "Don't forget, we need all the information we can get."

Brenna nodded. When Rose was out of the room, she murmured, "Like I could I forget."

Fifteen minutes later everyone had a hot drink and a muffin, and the fireplace was pumping out waves of heat.

Still, the room felt different, Brenna thought. The sense of refuge from just last night had been destroyed by the events since. Unseen occupants had made their presence known. There was no safe haven left at Wisdom Court.

Max had an oversized book serving as a lap desk and was sorting through his notes. "Before we continue reading the journal, I'd like to hear more about how you found it." He glanced at Rose. "You said you were directed to it. What did you mean?"

Rose described the bitter cold on the second floor and the shaft of light shining toward the end of the attic stair step. How the keyhole at the center of the brass circle was made visible, allowing her later to use the tiny key she'd found in Caldicott's room. "I'd never noticed those circles until then."

Max wrote down the details and then regarded her. "Was there anything else you can recall? Sounds? Odors?"

"I did hear a buzzing sound," Rose said. "That was how it started. For a moment I thought a bee or wasp might be trapped at one of the windows. Before I could look, the light intensified and eventually focused onto the brass disk. Then the cold drove me downstairs."

"I've encountered buzzing associated with manifestations. Interesting." Max scribbled on the paper and glanced back at her. "Did you have any sense as to the intent behind the actions of the…entity? That it meant you to find that step?"

Rose rubbed at her temples. "I'm not certain of anything right now, Max. All I can tell you is what happened. The intent behind it is beyond me."

For a moment Max appeared at a loss. "I'm sorry, I realize you reacted to the stimuli imposed upon you." He added carefully, "I'm attempting to categorize the events. So much is happening here, and with far greater intensity than any of the hauntings I've investigated. It's difficult to find a way to grasp them. What I should have asked was, did you perceive anything else that might expand our comprehension of the phenomenon?"

"No." Rose sighed. "I was so…weakened by that dreadful cold…"

"Hmmm. Similar to what we felt in the kitchen?"

"Maybe." Rose frowned, considering. "It's hard to say. The rest of you were in the kitchen and that made it easier to bear."

"Brenna was alone last night when she experienced a visitation." Andrea's chin was tilted at stubborn angle. "She had a hard time of it."

Kerry set down her cup. "What are you talking about?"

"Andrea…" Brenna scowled at her and waved a hand at Max's questioning look. "I guess the spirit made the rounds last night, but for me it was almost all sound effects." She repeated the particulars of her battle in the dark hallway to get into her rooms. "Every sound I made reverberated until I thought I'd go deaf. It wasn't cold or anything, and I couldn't see because of the dark. No odors, but I'm not sure I'd have noticed them anyway. I was pretty scared."

Aura Lee looked worried. "Could you pick out any specific words in all the noise? Like chanting?"

Brenna shook her head. "It all seemed to come from

me, the clang of the keys dropping, the sound from hitting the wall. It was like being in some out-of-whack echo chamber."

"And what time was it?" Max was writing swiftly.

Brenna glanced at Andrea. "Do you remember when you left my place?"

"After midnight for sure." Andrea thought for a moment. "It was twenty till one when I turned out my light."

Max looked up from his notes with a grin. "This is astonishing. I've never come upon so many clearly defined manifestations."

"We're so happy to provide you with material." Noreen's tone was acidic.

Max ignored her. "Have you experienced anything else?" He asked Brenna.

She looked down at her hands, realizing how much more she had to tell. "I've had dreams since my grandmother died earlier this year, but they've become crazy vivid and much scarier since I got to Wisdom Court. Then there's the stars added to my film, and the weird fortune cookie message. And the face in the attic window—I've taken several pictures of that."

"Don't forget the star on your bathroom mirror," Andrea added.

"Oh, yeah." Brenna half-laughed. "Can't forget that."

When no one said anything, Brenna glanced around, finding herself the target of uneasy stares.

Aura Lee's hands were clasped together in her lap and her eyes were saucer-wide. "On your mirror?"

Brenna leaned against the back of the chair, aware suddenly of just how tired she felt. "Drawn in the steam after I took a shower."

"How long have these things been happening?" Max

had lost his air of scholarly enjoyment and looked thoroughly uncomfortable.

"As soon as I got here. Five, six days ago?"

"When were you going to mention all this?" Rose asked.

"When there was a pause in the action." Brenna winced at the sharp edge to her voice. "Look, I wasn't hiding it or anything. You know it's been loony-toons ever since I got here."

"Is that all of it?" Max asked slowly. "What you told us?"

"I guess so." Brenna rubbed one brow, trying to recall the details of her time. "Yeah, that's it. It's been pretty intense."

"Beware the face of the Observer, for its placid surface hides maelstroms and nameless dangers," Noreen stated, her voice deep. "Marcella DePugh Wallace. Eighteen thirteen to eighteen seventy-two."

Rose blinked. "You must be thawing out."

Noreen smirked. "I'm happy to report that I am."

Brenna rubbed at her head irritably, and coughed at the thickening air. "Do you smell lavender?"

"Cottie wore lavender," Aura Lee murmured. "I smell it, too." She sniffed and dabbed at her eyes with her handkerchief.

"Always?" Max was frowning at his notes.

"No, sometimes she wore more of a cinnamon perfume." Aura Lee took an eager look into the corners of the room. "Do you think she might be here?"

"I suppose she might." Max breathed in deeply. "The scent is quite strong, isn't it? Almost unpleasant."

"Ur-gent." The word was more croaked than spoken, the voice uttering it harsh and low.

Max stiffened at the sound, his gaze veering to Rose. She was gaping at Kerry in horror. Beside her Aura Lee was in shock, hand on her chest, her mouth opening and shutting silently.

Brenna's breath was coming in gasps. She saw Max turn toward Kerry and extend his hand. At the brush of his fingers against her shoulder he jerked back in reflex, every ounce of color leaving his face, but forced himself to touch her again.

Kerry's eyes were closed, her facial muscles slack. Her head sagged to one shoulder and her arms flopped to her sides. "Must...know," said the voice coming from Kerry. Her lips did not move. "Danger."

Kerry slumped against Max and his arms went around her, clutching her against him. "Kerry, darling, are you all right? Kerry." He pulled back to look into her face and patted her cheeks, one after the other.

Noreen was on her feet. "Where's my phone? Where's yours?" she demanded of Andrea.

Rose was statue-still, gaze fixed on Kerry. Brenna lurched out of her chair to help her, afraid she, too, was going to collapse.

After a moment Kerry twitched and coughed. She pulled out of Max's hold and sucked in a deep breath, and then coughed again.

Aura Lee made a small sound and slid off the sofa onto the floor.

CHAPTER 21

"Aura Lee!" Rose knelt at her side, peering into her face, patting her hand. She put her ear to her chest. "Her breathing's slow but steady."

"Should we get the doctor over here?" Noreen let out a breath. "And if we do, what do we tell her?"

"Kerry." Max held her across his lap and had her head against his chest. "Luv, wake up." He bent to look more closely at her. "Kerry, wake up. She's pale as death." He looked in appeal toward Noreen. "I've never seen someone go right out like this. Usually they recover after the spirit leaves them." He ran a finger over her cheek.

"How do you know it has?" Brenna and Andrea had reached for each other's hands and were holding on for dear life. "Maybe who—whatever is still there," Brenna said, shivering even as she said the words. "How do you tell?"

Rose got to her feet. "I'll call Jerri. We'll have to tell her some of what's been going on, but she'll be discreet, I think." Hurrying out of the room, she turned back to summon Andrea and Brenna. "You two get some hot water and hand towels. Wipe their faces and their hands. It might help revive them."

Brenna and Andrea followed her out.

Noreen bent to rest one palm on Aura Lee's forehead. "She has a normal temperature, I think. She looks as though she's sleeping." With difficulty she stood up and made her way to Max's side. "Is the girl breathing freely?"

Max nodded, tightening his hold on her.

"How much more can we take of this horror show?" Noreen sat down on the edge of the cushion. "It's getting worse, and quickly. If Kerry was actually channeling some entity, what comes next?"

Kerry made a sound, a long sigh, and moved her head.

Max bent over her, cupping her cheek gently. "Kerry, can you hear me? Kerry," he repeated more loudly. "Wake up, luv."

Eyes opening slowly, Kerry looked up at Max in confusion. "What happened?"

Max's breath whooshed out in a relieved sigh. "Thank God. I was getting worried." He stroked her hair back from her forehead. "You were in a trance, luv, speaking for the dead. How do you feel?"

"What?" Kerry struggled to get up, and with Max's help, finally managed to sit leaning against him. "You're saying I was possessed? Are you delusional?" She gazed around, seeing Noreen sitting on the other side. "Has he been drinking?"

Noreen's chuckle was shaky. "Believe what he says, my dear. You gave voice to something—we're not sure what. Scared us all."

Kerry rubbed at her brow and grimaced. "I have a horrible headache." She glanced down at the floor as Andrea came into the room with a basin of water and several washcloths. "What's wrong with Aura Lee?"

Andrea dipped a cloth into the water and wrung it

out, placing it with care across Aura Lee's forehead. "She fainted and fell off the couch when you started speaking in tongues. Rose is calling the doctor."

Brenna appeared with a second bowl and came to the sofa to sit beside Kerry. The water sloshed near the edge of the bowl. "Careful, I don't want to get you wet. I'm glad to see you're awake." She got the cloth wet and surveyed Kerry. "Let me sponge your face and hands. Rose told me to," she added as Kerry began to protest. "She'll get mad at me if I don't follow orders."

"Right." Kerry submitted to Brenna's efforts and rested against Max. "What did I say?"

Max settled her more comfortably beside him and peered into her face. "You look a bit more among the living. You said *urgent* and *must know.* Then, *danger.* Do you remember doing it?"

Kerry shook her head, wincing and putting her hand to her eyes again. "The last thing I remember is drinking hot chocolate and waiting for the fire to warm me up."

"Rose?" Aura Lee said in a faint voice.

Andrea dabbed more warm water across her face. "Are you awake? Can you hear me?"

"I hear you. Where's Rose?"

Rounding the doorway, Rose hurried toward Aura Lee. "You're awake! Thank goodness for that. Jerri will be here soon to make sure you're all right."

Aura Lee made an effort to turn to her side, but Rose pressed on her shoulder and eased her back to the rug. "Jerri said to keep you from moving until she can make sure you haven't hurt yourself. You just relax. Hand me a blanket, will you?" she said to Noreen. "Thanks." She tucked the soft green folds around Aura Lee's neck and made sure she was warm. "How's Kerry?"

"Headache, some disorientation," said Max. "No memory of the event."

Kerry opened her eyes. "You've got your three-piece suit voice again. I'm okay," she said to Rose. "Sorry for the drama."

"Don't be silly. It's not as though you did it deliberately, not you."

Kerry smiled up at Max. "Good thing I'm a skeptic, right? Best defense against being thought a fake," she murmured. She sagged more deeply against him and her eyes closed.

"Max?" Rose's voice rose in concern.

He peered at her and he put his hand to her face. He looked at Rose. "Asleep."

"I'll feel a lot better after Jerri checks them out." Rose shot a look of concern at Aura Lee, who was examining the room as if it were strange to her. "What are we going to do about all this?" she asked abruptly. "What are we going to do?"

The doctor came and soon went, having pronounced both Aura Lee and Kerry shaken but essentially undamaged. "You, however," Jerri Williamson said bluntly to Rose, "look like a stiff wind would blow you into the next county. I get your rigmarole about not wanting to go into detail, but whatever's going on here is taking its toll on all of you. The only way you keep me from digging into those details is to promise to keep a close eye on everyone, especially the elders." The cynical smile didn't sit well on the square, jolly face that kept her one of the most popular doctors in the city. "I mean it, take care of yourself and watch out for the others. I'll check back in a few days and there'll be hell to pay if you ignore my excellent advice."

With that she drove away in her ancient Citroen, its

exhaust belching smoke into Boulder's heavily monitored air. For the hundredth time Rose wondered how many air pollution violations she'd accumulated over the years.

Rose turned and went back into the house. She was thinking about lunch when she entered the living room where everyone still sat. Noreen was nodding over a book and Brenna was listening to Andrea. She glanced up from her tablet when Rose sat down in the chair beside her.

Max was continuing to act as a pillow for Kerry. "Where do we stand?"

Rose surveyed the motley group with affection. "I'm thinking that we haven't had lunch, and after we eat, maybe we should all take a nap. What do you think?"

Andrea sighed. "I hate to say it, but I think we ought to keep reading Caldicott's journal. I don't know about you, but I want to get to the bottom of this paranormal stuff as soon as we can."

Brenna nodded her agreement. "If there's any information in it that can put a stop to the creepy-crawly stuff around here, I'm all for it."

Rose looked at Aura Lee, who was ensconced in her favorite chair, still wrapped in a fluffy throw. "Agreed. I'm tired but I couldn't sleep now anyway."

"Kerry will kill us if she doesn't get to do the reading."

"No she won't," said Kerry, her eyes still shut. "Let somebody else read it for a while. I'll just listen."

"Noreen? How say you?"

"*We are begun on a great quest and I shall not be of the lesser sort who would impede us.* Lilliana Salter Lunderson, 1871-1922."

"Wonder what her quest was?" Kerry mumbled.

"Haven't a clue, my dear." Noreen shifted her

weight to sit more erectly. "But I'm in agreement with her."

Rose stood up. "All right, I'm going to order pizza—the cheesier and more fat-laden the better. Brenna, vegetarian for you, and the rest of you can fight over what I choose."

"No anchovies," called Kerry as Rose headed for the kitchen.

"On the side," she answered.

They elected Max to continue the reading after the pizza had been inhaled. He sat nearer the light at one end of the sofa and opened Caldicott's journal to the marked page.

"We'd reached the bit where she says the establishment of Wisdom Court was a result of her love story, to say nothing of Duncan's Nazi-loving father," reminded Max.

"Which sounds pretty melodramatic, when you think about it," Brenna said.

"We'll see." Max began to read.

> *That spring was a time out of time I could never regret. Duncan and I were bent on making every moment count for the time we might never have together. We met at an abandoned cottage tucked into a copse on the far edge of his father's estate. Vacant since the death of the groundskeeper years before, it became our secret place. Duncan hadn't returned to Oxford, but instead was settling his affairs before enlisting. I'd been distressed he hadn't introduced me to his father, thinking it was because of my background, but when I asked him, his response shook me. "More like you should be upset about my background. My*

father is doing all he can to keep England from going to war with Germany."

He told me visitors to the estate were arriving in darkness and kept isolated from everyone, including the servants. Duncan believed some were go-betweens from the German government. "My father believes in Hitler's positions and that England should join with his government to prevent economic disaster in Europe." We were huddled near the small peat fire, wrapped in a blanket, careful to use little light for fear of discovery.

"He's supporting a clandestine effort," he said in a near-whisper. "He's been at me again to travel with him to Berlin to further the scheme."

"It's mad," I murmured, "and traitorous as well. Won't the authorities discover what he's doing?"

Duncan leaned his head against mine. "I'll try to reason with him when he returns tonight. He's acting in opposition to everything I believe. If I have to stop him, I shall, but I don't want him to know about us. I fear what he might do if he thinks he could influence me through you."

Later that week, it was a different Duncan who met me. I'd never seen him without the calm that was so attractive. That night, however, he was nervous, almost fearful, looking over his shoulder as we settled onto the old chair before the fire. "My father has become an occultist," he said quietly. "He believes he and his cronies can bring about England's refusal to go to war by way of spells and objects consecrated to the devil."

I looked at him, bewildered. "Are you talking about magic?"

Duncan nodded. "He's accumulated an array of potions and crystals, and was boasting of having obtained a powerful talisman capable of amplifying the powers he's discovered in himself. He's been corresponding with that blighter Crowley and his sort, and refuses to consider anything I say against it."

We held each other like children in a storm. "I must get you out of the village, dearest. He knows I'm seeing someone, and mentioned it. He wants to know who you are, I know, in order to use you to force me to do his bidding. Get your things together and be ready to leave within three days. I can't do what's necessary if I have to worry about your safety."

"When shall I leave?" I'd known since our first meeting we'd be parted, but I'd planned to stay in the village with Flo after he was gone.

"Any time now. I'm working on getting you out of the country." He seemed angry at my shock. "Don't you understand? He's dangerous. He still has entrée into certain circles of power. I won't risk your safety, Clara. You must trust me."

I packed what few things I had, clothing and a few mementoes of Mum and hid them at the cottage. Duncan told me not to share with Flo my plans to leave.

"But where can I go?" I asked Duncan in despair. "You'll be in the RAF. Can't I go to

London to work and wait for you?"

He pulled me to him and held me so tightly I could scarcely breathe. "We found a body yesterday...a Gypsy girl, the cousin of my friend Andras. She'd been used in a ritual, a sacrifice. God!" He swore violently. "These scum are living in the Dark Ages, casting curses and praying to evil spirits." He shook me by the shoulders, leaving bruises with his strong hands. "I'll see they pay for what they've done, but I won't leave you here to suffer something of the same."

The next night I arrived at the cottage and in the clearing I found a young man. Clad in shabby clothing, he was waiting beside a horse hitched to a caravan. I started to run away but he spoke. "Stay, please. I am Andras, Duncan's friend. He asked me to meet him here." He rubbed the horse's nose and pulled its ear gently. "This is Firefly."

I turned back to him. In the moonlight I could see sorrow in his face, and kindness.

I stepped toward him, hand extended. "I'm Clara."

His smile was quite beautiful.

Moments later Duncan pushed through the thicket at the edge of the clearing. He was out of breath, carrying a leather valise. He glanced behind him, searching to see if anyone followed. He set the valise in front of me and turned to Andras.

"I regret being late, my friend. I ran into a spot of bother." He shifted his left arm and I saw with horror the patch of blood on his shoulder where the seam of his coat was torn.

"Duncan, you're hurt!" I moved toward him, wanting to look at his wound, but he took my hand and held me beside him.

"Later, my dear." He looked again at his friend. "I'd hoped for more time, but you must go now. They may have discovered which way I went."

Andras nodded and walked to the horse, loosing a rope from a branch of the thicket and running his hand along the back of the creature.

Duncan bent to pick up the valise. "Let's get your things." As we entered the cottage he dropped it beside the door. "Listen, darling." He took me in his arms, and I could smell the sweat and blood on his shirt. "In the valise are bearer bonds, a good deal of them. They'll be enough to keep you until I catch up with you later on. I put in fifty pounds for the journey." He leaned his cheek against my hair and stroked my back. "Andras will take you to the edge of London." He mentioned the name of a village on the city outskirts. "My friend, David—we were at Oxford together—is the son of an American diplomat. He'll see you to their embassy and get you on the first airplane going to New York."

"But, Duncan," I said in protest, "I have no passport. I can't just—"

"Hush." He went still, listening intently. After a moment he resumed his instructions. "Everything has been taken care of. In the valise are addresses of two banks in New York where you can stow the bonds, half in each. Don't say a word about them, not to Andras, *not to David, not to anyone." His mouth brushed against my cheeks, one then the other. He pulled away to look into my face, concern in his eyes. "We haven't had enough time." He bent his head and kissed me deeply. "No matter. I couldn't love you more if we'd had a lifetime. You are the other half of me." He kissed me again and looked at me, tears in his eyes. "If I survive, I'll find you. Wait for me."*

"Forever." I threw myself into his arms and we held desperately to one another until he pushed me away and left the cottage. He walked quickly to Andras. He said a few words and the two men clasped each other in a swift hug. He moved round the caravan into the thicket.

Andras came to the door. "We must go, Clara. Are these your things?" I nodded and he lifted my bag and the valise, carrying them to the caravan and thrusting them inside. He took me by one arm and guided me up the steps and into the caravan. It smelled of cinnamon and wood smoke. "Let me in next to you," he said, and climbed inside, the vehicle swaying with his movements. He picked up the edge of a rug and ran his hand along the corner of the bench beside it. With a metallic click a door opened to a compartment under the floor. "You must get in and you must be silent. Don't use the torch unless I say you may."

I glanced out the door in time to see Duncan cutting a branch from a bush. He began to sweep the ground near the cottage and I realized he was trying to eliminate our tracks.

"It must be now, Clara," said Andras.

I lowered myself into the compartment and onto a mattress. Blankets, a flask of water, and a parcel of food were at the edge of the bed alongside the torch. Andras set the bag and the valise at my feet and closed the door above me, enclosing me in darkness but for a tiny bit of light through a crack near my head. I heard the rug as he slid it into place over the trap door. I felt the caravan sway again and imagined Andras climbing onto the seat in front.

The caravan jerked ahead and slowly we began to move forward. I shifted to try peering through the crack but could see nothing. I was leaving Duncan and I couldn't see him, couldn't wave to him. Panic swept through me at the thought of never seeing him again. I wanted to scream to him, to demand that Andras let me out of the box, but I clung to what Duncan wanted of me. He would challenge his father and perhaps turn him over to the authorities. If I let myself be vulnerable, it could harm Duncan. The one thing I could do for him was to keep myself safe.

I turned onto my side to look at the light shining through the crack in the wood. I let my tears come silently.

"Goodbye, my love," I whispered. "Goodbye."

CHAPTER 22

I wept until I fell asleep. When I awoke, I realized we had stopped. I looked for the small bit of light from the crack in the corner, but could see nothing. It was still night.

When I heard the door open and felt the sway as someone came onto the caravan I was uneasy. The sound of the rug being moved and the click of the lock to the compartment terrified me. I tensed, ready to fight, but found myself looking up at Andras in the light of a lantern. He put his finger to his lips and extended his hand to help me get out, whispering an explanation.

"We're outside my people's camp. I didn't want you to wake and not know this. Come with me to the edge of the woods to wait and I will approach to make certain it is safe to go on."

I was glad to move about and be in the fresh air. When he came back he waved at me and led me to a clearing where people sat around a large campfire. Andras led me to a wiry man who stood up as I came closer. I could see the resemblance between them, and he was introduced to me as his father, Peter. Andras spoke with him in a language I didn't understand. He eyed me with some suspicion and gestured to the woman seated on the rock beside him. "My wife will help you, miss." With that he turned back to the fire and spoke to one of the men nearby.

Andras made me known to his mother, Miriam, and she invited me to her caravan to talk privately. There she offered me food and wine and asked Andras and me to sit by the small fire, burnt down to glowing coals.

"You are in trouble, my child." It was not a question. When I nodded, she glanced at her son and spoke in the language her husband had used.

Andras got to his feet and said, "I will return in a moment."

Miriam lit a cigarette and smoked silently as I ate the spicy soup she'd given me. When I had finished, she took my plate and asked to see my hand.

"I beg your pardon?"

"I wish to see your palm, my child." Her dark eyes gleamed with amusement. "Have you never met a Gypsy fortuneteller?"

Embarrassed, I extended my hand.

She took it and drew her fingers across my palm. Her skin was cool to the touch and gave me a feeling of safety. But before I could relax into that comfort, her face changed, lines deepening, eyes widening. She looked from my palm to my eyes, searching.

"What is it?" I pulled my hand from hers and clenched it into a fist.

From the large campfire behind us came music and Miriam turned toward it. When she looked back round at me, her face was smooth again, her eyes shuttered. Andras was coming toward us, carrying the valise Duncan had given me.

I stumbled to my feet, afraid at his expression. "What are you doing with that?" My voice was tremulous. "Duncan said to keep it in the caravan."

Andras spoke rapidly to his mother and placed the valise at my feet. "It is not about what you think." He pulled a parcel wrapped in brown paper from his coat pocket and put it into my hand. "This was on the top of the supplies Duncan gave you." He stared at me, narrowing his eyes and giving me a slight nod.

He was avoiding any mention of the bonds. I nodded and he turned to his mother. "Should she open it, Mama?"

Miriam looked at the package with fear. "First I must protect." She motioned to us. "Come with me."

She led us to the back of her caravan and went up the two steps, reaching inside to pull out a satchel. From it she drew a twist of paper tied with red string and sealed with black wax, a small bag, and a vial of liquid. She took the items to a nearby clearing and crouched near an open spot. "Put the package here."

I set it in the center of the place she indicated and stepped back.

She held out the twist and told me to break the wax seal. When I had done so, she unwound the red string and opened the twist, sprinkling its contents in a circle around the object, chanting words I didn't understand throughout. She put drops at four different places in the circle, repeating words monotonously. Then she scattered what appeared to be dried leaves over the area. She told me to remove the paper from the object. As I did so she continuously spoke in prayerful tones.

"See what it is."

Inside the circle was a black stone, roughly triangular in shape. As I looked at it, a point of red light began to shine at the center. The light grew into a glowing oval of deep red.

Miriam had paled and appeared almost wizened. "Wrap it in the paper," she said harshly.

My hand shaking, I picked up the stone and dropped it again. "It's hot!" My fingers and thumb were red with welts.

"Use the paper. Wrap it." Her voice was so guttural I could hardly understand.

Working as fast as I could, I wrapped the stone in the paper and set it down in the circle once more.

Miriam took a match from her pocket and held it to a black chunk of wax, dripping it over the parcel, sealing the paper shut. "You

*must take that away from here." Her eyes met
mine and I flinched at the wild fear in them.
"It is under a protective spell, but I will not
have it here. It was given to you?"*

*I wondered. Duncan had given me the
valise, so in that way it had been given to me.
I nodded.*

*"Who gave it to you either did not know its
evil or wished you harm. I do not think you
are one who would pass on harm to someone
else. You cannot escape it. It is yours and you
must make certain you are protected against
it. The spell I cast will last for some time, but
not forever."*

*Andras took my arm. "Clara, if we are to
meet Duncan's friend, we must go. Now."*

*I picked up the package and put it into the
valise. Soon we were on our way toward the
village where David awaited me. Back again
in the dark compartment, I shivered at the
memory of the terror in Miriam's eyes. At my
feet was the valise with the stone that had
caused it.*

*I found sleep impossible for a very long
time.*

Tears slid down Aura Lee's cheeks. Noreen got out
of her chair to go to her. "Now, now." Her low voice
was choked with emotion. She patted Aura Lee's
shoulder. "Now, now."

Max and Kerry were holding onto each other and
Brenna dabbed at her eyes with a tissue. Rose and
Andrea just looked at each other. "Another call for
brandy?" Andrea asked.

Rose nodded.

"How did she live through it?" Kerry wondered. "She and Duncan were so happy and then the world came to an end." She leaned her forehead against Max's shoulder. "And then the whole business about the weird stone and the spell. I don't think I could bear it."

Rose straightened her shoulders and sniffed mightily. "You'd be surprised what you can bear. We all get our turn in the shooting gallery, as a target or as a marksman. Or both."

Noreen wiped her eyes. "I might have to add that to the collection." She produced a watery smile. "Very worthy."

Aura Lee pushed herself out of her chair. "I made lemon bars this morning. We need dessert." She started out of the room and then turned back. "Was that the end of the journal?"

Max looked down at the volume. "Yes. I was hoping for more information. We need help in dealing with the things happening here."

"Should you be up?" Rose asked Aura Lee.

Aura Lee looked puzzled for a moment and then smiled. "You know, I forgot all about myself. I think I'm all right."

"Let me help you." She followed Aura Lee into the kitchen. She put her arm around the older woman's shoulders and hugged her gently.

Andrea got up to fetch glasses and the brandy bottle. "I'm afraid to find out what happened to Duncan. If she never mentioned him in all her years at Wisdom Court, the odds aren't good that she ever saw him again."

Max stood up and reached a hand to pull Kerry to her feet. "How're you feeling, luv?"

Kerry wiped her cheeks with the backs of her hands. "I'm so sad I could curl up, and I don't know if I've ever been so tired before, but other than that, I guess I'll live." She leaned against Max and looked into his eyes. "Want to escort me to the bathroom? I'd just as soon not wander around on my own for a while."

"More than happy to comply." He took her by the hand and led her toward the hallway.

Noreen watched them go with a half-smile. "I'd like to see that pairing continue. I've never seen Kerry so *smooth* before."

Andrea was setting highball glasses in strategic places and filling them as she went. "It's good to see her happy. She deserves to be." She placed a glass at Brenna's elbow. "You're very quiet. Deep thoughts?"

Brenna shook her head. "I'm missing my boyfriend. There's nothing like an unhappy love story to make you miss the one you love."

Andrea filled her glass. "I'm tempted to call Neal and have him stop by. I would if it wouldn't take so much time to bring him up to date as to what's happened. I'm not willing to wait that long. I'll call him after we've finished."

"Lucky." Brenna looked at the cell phone she'd taken out of her pocket. "I'll call Dink, too, but I wish I could see him."

Andrea patted her shoulder. "I feel your pain."

CHAPTER 23

"This volume can't be the end of Ms. Wyntham's journal, can it?" Max tapped it with one finger. "There's so much more we need to know."

"It's the only one we've found." Kerry leaned against his shoulder. "And we've looked everywhere. Unless we get another visitation or some ghostly signposts, this is it."

Noreen finished chewing her last lemon bar and dabbed at her mouth with a napkin. "We haven't taken apart the other stair steps. Now that we have this one, we can be more thorough in our search."

Rose stared at the portrait of Caldicott over the fireplace. "To think of what she went through. I can't stand not knowing if Duncan ever found her or how she ended up in Colorado." She shivered. "And what happened to the odd stone the fortuneteller put under the protection spell?"

Brenna was lying on the floor, wrapped in a fuzzy throw. "What bothers me is we still don't know about what's going on here at Wisdom Court. I don't think anything in the journal explained the hauntings. Are we any closer to understanding what's behind the strange things we've all experienced?"

Aura Lee glanced down at her. "We might have a few more clues. Duncan told her about the talisman his father bragged about, that it could amplify his powers and the powers of his evil group. Don't you think the stone Andras found in the valise is probably that talisman?"

"It's a reasonable assumption." Max thumbed back through the pages of the journal. "There's no description of it before they reached the Gypsy camp, but Miriam certainly tumbled to its presence and power. She must have told Andras to bring the valise to her. Why else would he have fetched it?"

Kerry read along with Max to the end of the page. "When Miriam put the protective spell on the stone she said her ritual would last for a time, but not forever. It's possible Caldicott brought the talisman here, to Wisdom Court. She wouldn't have palmed it off on someone else—Miriam had that part right. So what if it's still here? What if it's powerful and is affecting what happens here?"

"What a cheerful thought." Rose rubbed her hands together, finally blowing on fingers. "I'm cold," she said at Kerry's worried expression. "I honestly wonder if I'll ever get warm again after today." She propped her feet on the coffee table and looked at Max. "Do you have any notion of what spell Miriam could have used? For that matter, do you know anything about Gypsy beliefs?"

"Little beyond some of the more hackneyed representations in popular media, and I've read several books written by sociologists regarding the Irish Travellers. It's difficult to study either the Travellers or the Romani because they so distrust outsiders. And who can blame them? In order to be certain of which group Andras and Miriam belonged to I'd have to create a family tree for them, hunt for whatever branch exists now, and gain their trust. And, after all, it's been seventy-some years since that meeting at the encampment."

"What about Duncan's family?" Andrea was doodling in her notebook. "I know Caldicott worked hard to mask their identities, but wouldn't it be possible to trace them? Or the diplomat whose son was to help Clara," she added in excitement. "Maybe *their* family has passed down the legend of David's involvement in getting Clara out of England. I wonder if we could possibly find them."

"I don't know about this," Aura Lee said in a troubled voice. "Cottie went to a lot of trouble to hide all of this information from everyone." She shot an anxious look at Andrea. "*Everyone*. We've experienced some amazing things here over the last few months. What if, by trying to find answers to our questions, we brought attention to Wisdom Court?"

"You mean by rocking the boat we might create ripples that could be followed back to us?" Noreen asked slowly. Her gaze met Rose's worried eyes and looked back to Aura Lee. "That might sound a bit paranoid, but it deserves some thought."

Max brought his arm around Kerry's shoulder and leaned against the sofa back. "People die over time but evil lives on. I wouldn't like to go up against someone like Duncan's father or his kind. Somehow, without tipping anyone off to our interest, we need to discover whether any sort of neo-Nazi group has carried on, continuing the activities begun just before the war." He rested his head against Kerry's hair. "Aura Lee, you're a very wise woman. And you bake like an angel."

Aura Lee blushed with pleasure.

"You know," Rose said slowly, "I think we'd better

redouble our efforts here before we tackle the English side of things. That means checking possible hidey-holes—all of the attic stairs, for instance—and other possibilities in the house. Maybe hidden spaces in cupboards or other built-ins. Just listening to what Cottie wrote about the secret compartment in the caravan got me thinking about that possibility. You're the architecture nut, Brenna. You can help us figure out where such things could be hidden, in the house and the associate houses as well."

Brenna nodded. "Don't forget, we might get help from some of the other residents here. Well," she said in answer to Noreen's raised brows, "we've had more than a few nudges so far, haven't we?"

"I just wish those nudges didn't scare me so badly." Aura Lee clasped her hands together. "I feel like a failure as a mystical researcher thanks to becoming a babbling idiot every time something appears."

"Don't we all?" Rose stood up and stretched her arms over her head. "I don't know about the rest of you, but I need to move around a bit. And I'm ready to at least think about dinner. I'm in the mood for a salad after all the baked goods we've eaten the last few days. Anybody want to help me chop veggies?"

"I'm game." Brenna got up off the floor and folded up the throw, tossing it into the basket.

"Me, too." Andrea began to gather up plates and cups. "I don't know why I haven't gained twenty pounds since I first got here. All I do is eat and drink."

Aura Lee looked at them, a wise expression on her face. "I assume you've never heard about the haunting diet? I'm quite serious," she said and they stopped laughing. "It's a proven fact that working among those on the Other Side burns an enormous number of calories."

"I suspect there's a diet book in that, my dear, if

someone hasn't already written it." Noreen patted her shoulder as she went toward the kitchen. "I have my doubts about the willingness of dieters to saddle themselves with a passel of ghosts to lose weight. Although, when you think about it, there've been stranger diets than that one."

They went out of the room chuckling and arguing over what to fix for lunch. Caldicott's journal was left behind on the coffee table. As the sound of voices faded, the top cover moved upward and the pages riffled, slowly and then in rapid succession, as if turned by an impatient hand.

They ate the salad as an early dinner.

"Why do I keep thinking about baked potatoes slathered in sour cream *and* butter?" Noreen's voice was plaintive. "Not that I didn't like the salad," she added hastily. "It was delicious and it made me feel virtuous."

"I don't know about that," Rose said, tongue in cheek. "You drizzled a lot of ranch dressing on those righteous veggies."

"A garment of Virtue ne'er fits well when altered by ill-advised allowances made in the fabric of integrity."

Kerry nearly choked on her iced tea. "Tell me she's *not* a moralizing seamstress!"

Noreen's eyes twinkled. "Elizabeth Goodhue Rush, 1793-1862. She married above her station and spent her life trying to make up for it through moral turpitude and intellectual striving."

Max wandered into the room, smiling at their laughter. He set the three thick books he carried onto the sideboard. "You sound in good spirits."

"No pun intended?" Kerry shot him a flirtatious glance.

He grabbed her by the shoulders and gave her a smacking kiss and she slid her arms up his back and hugged him.

Aura Lee, sorting forks and knives into the sideboard flatware drawer, beamed at the two of them.

"Has Brenna returned?" Max asked. She'd gone for her camera and one of her architecture books.

"Not yet." Rose was making sure she had both a Phillips head and a blade screwdriver in her toolbox. "Did you find anything useful in the books or are you weightlifting?"

Max shook his head. "One is a history of Boulder, especially regarding more significant buildings. I'd hoped to find references to oddness or strange things happening at or around Wisdom Court. No luck, I'm afraid."

Noreen pulled on the reading glasses hanging at her neck and picked up a volume. "We're working under a disadvantage. People rarely mention supernatural events or rumors when they're writing histories. I suppose they want to be taken seriously."

"Indeed." Max took the book from her and opened it to a certain page, indicating a particular paragraph.

"The Stanley Thornton home at the base of Flagstaff Mountain is a large example of a four-square house with Queen Anne elements."

"That means we'll have plenty of places to search for hollow molding and such. The stair step where you found the journal was an inspired choice. It's a place seen but not seen, totally taken for granted." Max picked up another volume. "This one talks about ghosts at the Boulderado Hotel, but there's nothing I could find regarding hauntings at private residences."

"May I see?" Kerry took the book and looked at the copyright date. "This was published in 1932." She pursed her lips. "Caldicott didn't buy this house until

1955, meaning she didn't bring the evil stone—or talisman," she responded at Andrea's snicker, "until at least then. And that raises another question about our experience with Andrea's channeling Kelvin Haslett. He was at this house in 1908, long before Caldicott arrived here." She looked meaningfully at Rose. "That means the haunting tendencies existed much earlier."

Max was hunting for the copyright date in the third book. "This one came out in the early forties. You might be right, luv. The other possibility is when Caldicott came here with the talisman, she provided energy for—or opened a portal to—paranormal activity that continues today."

Aura Lee was shaking her head in doubt. "I don't understand how that could be the case. Before Andrea arrived we didn't have any signs of ghosts. I was looking for them! It wasn't until Andrea started drawing Kelvin that I knew something otherworldly was happening."

"But why were you looking for them?" Max stacked the books in place, looking at her with interest. "Had you sensed something? Perhaps a presence?"

"That's called leading the witness," Noreen said in a dry voice.

Max raised a brow. "It's a legitimate question. One usually becomes interested in a topic because of a specific event or an ingrained tendency. Was it because of your name? Aura Lee is rather a spiritual one," he added.

Understanding dawned. "Oh, no, dear. My given name is Aurelia. I began calling myself Aura Lee after I took my first class in spell casting." She beamed at him. "It seemed like a more *relevant* name."

"Ah, I see." Max nodded solemnly but his lips twitched. He cleared his throat. "Had you always wanted to study such things?"

"Well, yes and no. Let me see." She stared at the table, tapping her lips with one finger. "Oh, I remember! It was the year we had a new roof put on the house. After the work was finished, Cottie complained about sounds coming from upstairs, waking her in the night. A wise-woman I knew said renovations could upset the ghosts in a house, and the idea intrigued me. I started reading about hauntings and remedies and got more and more interested."

"Did the sounds continue?" Kerry asked.

"No, and I actually think I got rid of them, because I started a class on herbs and was practicing sage cleansings and the knocking stopped after that."

"And was Caldicott impressed?" Rose asked.

Aura Lee nodded proudly. "She told me I should keep taking classes. So I did."

"Well." Max shifted the stack of books minutely and looked at the others. "I suppose we'd best continue in our search, both for more information about Wisdom Court itself and for Ms. Wyntham's journals. It's difficult for me to believe she would write one volume and then stop. She had information she knew had to be shared. My theory is that she hid it somewhere on the property. All we need to do is find it."

Kerry gasped and swiveled in her chair, looking behind her. "Did you feel that?" Her green eyes were wide with surprise.

"Feel what?" Rose looked around the room.

"Something touched me." Kerry stood up and moved around the table toward Max. "I swear, somebody put a hand on my shoulder."

Brenna strode through the associate house hallway to her front door. When her key slid into the lock and turned easily, she opened the door with a sigh of relief, slipping inside and locking it once more. Setting the key on the foyer table, she saw her hand was trembling. *Okay, I find the book and get my camera. Then I'm out of here.*

Her books were on the shelves in the screening room. She flicked the light switch as she entered and had a fleeting sense that something was different but the thought faded before she could identify what she'd felt. It took several minutes to find her reference book on ornamental woodwork, and by the time she had it, she was aware of an increasing edginess. *Time to go, time to go.*

As she went back into the living room her cell rang. She glanced at the number and stopped, punching the answer button. "Dink."

"Hey, babe, how's it going?"

Her hand tightened and she fought off the need to let every scary, horrible thing tumble from her lips. "Ah…it's been pretty hairy here. Lots of stuff going on." She couldn't even remember what she'd told him. *We talked yesterday, right?*

"You sound weird. Spacey. You sure you're okay?"

Brenna felt a tingle down her spine and started walking toward the stairs. "We found a journal, it belonged to the woman who started this place. What she wrote about freaked us out and we're trying to deal with some of the new info."

"What about your work?" Dink's voice was cutting in and out, tinny and fading.

"I haven't done much yet, with all the ghost stuff. It's been too crazy."

"Ghost stuff?" He sounded as if he was in a well.

She took the stairs up to the bedroom two at a time. At the top she walked into a cloud of scent and the familiarity of it almost brought her to her knees. Wind Song. Her grandmother's perfume.

Brenna breathed in the fragrance. "Gran?"

She barely heard Dink calling her name as her hand fell to her side. "Gran, are you here?"

The air began to chill.

CHAPTER 24

Max had his arms wrapped around Kerry, who couldn't stop shivering. "Though it goes against my training," he said lightly, "you most likely had a muscle spasm or one of those odd starts we all feel now and again."

Kerry shook her head. "I felt it as surely as I feel your arms now." She caught Aura Lee's eyes. "Does it feel colder in here to you?"

"Yes, it does." Aura Lee took a throw from the basket near the fireplace and wrapped it around her shoulders. Her gaze darted about, searching the shadows in the corners.

"You're scaring each other." Rose glanced at her watch. "I wish Brenna would get back here. She's been gone a long time for just picking up her book and camera."

"No doubt she was distracted by something," Noreen tut-tutted. "She'll be back soon."

Rose went into the kitchen and looked out the window but saw nothing but leaves blowing across the cobblestone courtyard. She went back to the living room and leaned in at the arch. "I don't see her. I'll go check to make sure she's okay."

Andrea glanced up from the book in her lap. "You want me to come along?"

"No, that's okay. I'm being mother-hennish. Can't help it. I'll be right back."

The wind had picked up even more, blowing its chilly breath down the neck of Rose's sweatshirt. Clouds were gathering over the Flatirons, quenching the afternoon sun. Rose shivered as she scanned the area. Something was wrong. She didn't know what it was, but her heart was pumping faster and she felt like running. Something dangerous had been near.

Rose took the steps to the associate house door two at a time and slid her key into the lock. Immediately she smelled an odd, metallic odor that made her cough.

"Brenna!" She ran to her door and grasped the knob. It was locked. "Brenna!" Her hands were shaking enough to hinder her using the key. Finally she pushed it in and turned it, shoving open the door. She almost tripped over Brenna's body, lying in a limp pile like a load of laundry.

Rose knelt beside her. "Brenna, Brenna." She patted her cheek, then turned her onto her back and placed her ear against her chest. When she heard the slow, slight beat, her breath whooshed out in relief.

"Oh, my God," Rose muttered. "Oh, my God." She speed-dialed the Wisdom Court number and waited in a fever of impatience for someone to answer. "Andrea, get over here—Brenna's place. She's unconscious. I'll call an ambulance and you call the fire department. I can't tell if there's a fire, but it smells strange and—just call them." She bent over Brenna once more.

Kerry watched the ambulance roar from the

courtyard, lights flashing. Rose had opted to ride to the hospital with Brenna, who was still objecting to the journey as the door slammed shut. The firemen had come and gone, somewhat upset at finding nothing related to a fire. "What in the world will happen next?"

"Take it out of the law," Aura Lee said quickly. Her eyes puckered with worry. "Don't ask a question like that. It's an invitation to the Universe to answer it. And you won't necessarily care for the response."

Kerry started to answer sharply, but thought better of it. For all she knew, Aura Lee might have a point. Life was getting way too weird. "I'll keep that in mind," she said. "Let's go take another look at Brenna's place. Rose wants us to see if we can find anything. Brenna was basically out of it. It would help if we could figure out what went on in there."

Aura Lee led the way up the stairs to the west associate house and pushed the door open. "Do you smell smoke?" Kerry asked as they entered the hallway.

"I smell something." Aura Lee sniffed several times. "Not much, but there's a tinge in the air, sort of like the ozone smell you get when there's an electrical short."

"Wonder what it could've come from." Kerry pushed open Brenna's door and went inside, eyes darting around the room. "It looks okay in here, but who knows?"

"I'll take the kitchen and you can check around here." Aura Lee brushed by the plants in the foyer and stopped beside the sofa. "Look at this."

"What?" Kerry went to her side and saw what appeared to be gray jelly on the back of the couch. "What is it, food? Did she take time for a snack, do you think?"

Aura Lee bent to the leather and sniffed directly above the substance. "Yuck, I hope not. It smells like a combination of bad wiring and rotten eggs."

Kerry saw more of the stuff on the floor. "Let's get a sandwich bag and pick it up. If nothing else, we can run it by Jerri, see if it's organic."

Aura Lee smiled. "It almost feels like we're on one of those forensic shows. You know, *CSI* or *Bones*."

"Yeah, I guess." Kerry peered more closely at the gloppy substance. "Bring a spoon or something, will you? I don't want to touch this."

Aura Lee headed for the kitchen and came back with a bag and a butter knife, along with a wad of paper towels she handed to Kerry. She scraped the knife across the leather back, getting most of the gluey mess, and stuck it in the bag along with it. "We don't want to destroy evidence."

"Right." Kerry had wiped up the mess on the floor and tossed it in the nearby wastebasket. She took the bag and turned toward the stairs. "I'll leave our evidence on the table here. See what you can find in the kitchen while I look upstairs, okay?"

"Okay."

Kerry set the bag down and went to the stairway, turning on the light switch. Nothing happened. "Huh." She glanced up the steps, hoping for some light at the top, but the shadows were deep and she couldn't make out anything on the landing. "Creepy," she muttered and started climbing, holding fast to the railing. She'd turn on the hall light when she got up there.

Halfway up she heard a soft thud and then another. She stopped. Listening as hard as she could, barely breathing, Kerry waited. As the moments ticked off, the hairs on the back of her neck rose. She looked over her shoulder and saw how far the stairs behind her extended back to the doorway to the living room.

Wait, it's not that far, that doesn't make any sense. Frozen air surrounded her, went through her, creeping into her bones, and she knew without doubt that if she had the light to see it, her breath would be as visible as smoke. She heard a creak on the stairs above her, like someone trying to sneak down ancient steps. *Time to get the hell out of here.*

Kerry tried to let go of the railing, tried to turn back toward the faraway foot of the stairwell.

Kerry, she told herself, lift your hand, raise your foot. C'mon get out!

She couldn't move.

She felt the cold settle inside her, curling up in her body, making her its permanent home.

She sank deeper into the frost.

Aura Lee stood in front of the kitchen windows, wondering why Brenna had taped Christmas wrapping paper across the lower panes. Not that the snowmen cavorting across the snowy landscape weren't cheerful, but Christmas was three months away. Was Brenna one of those people who celebrated the holiday all year long? "Ah well," she muttered, "no harm done."

Aura Lee wasn't quite sure what she was looking for. Brenna had been so confused about what had happened before she'd fainted. She couldn't recall anything specific that could have triggered the black out. *There isn't always a particular cause. Sometimes you just react to the energies in a room.* She thought of the sounds she'd heard in her bedroom and the fingers struggling to reach through her silver tray. *I wouldn't have minded fainting after that experience.*

Aura Lee looked along the countertops, half-expecting to find more of the gelatinous substance they'd bagged in the living room. Nothing. Opening a drawer at random, she rifled through napkins and placemats, and closed it again. The problem, as she saw it, was the subjective nature of receiving transmissions from spirits on the Other Side. Each person was prone to noticing certain things over others. Like tendencies in intellectual pursuits and what music a person preferred, the manifestations of the dead were apt to be detected by the living who shared their abilities and choices. It just made sense.

Aura Lee ran her fingers across the cupboard doors, stopping to open them and check their condition. All were neat and clean, so far. Brenna hadn't moved much of anything. Of course, she might be eating take-out every night, but it was only fair to take the evidence as it lay. Tidy cabinets usually meant a reasonable degree of cleanliness.

Aura Lee peered around the room, focusing on details. *Surely I can find a hint of something. Maybe cans disarranged on the shelves, like Rose's fountain rocks.* She shivered and pulled the edges of her sari up a little higher around her neck. The sun was currently shining, but the air inside was cold.

The pantry showed no evidence of supernatural messages in the way the cans were stacked. Aura Lee narrowed her eyes in thought. The kitchen was a bust. If any self-respecting shade had been at work, there'd be signs of occupancy. She hadn't heard anything, hadn't seen anything. An acrid scent drifted across her nostrils, the ozone odor again, stronger this time. Maybe there actually was a short in a wire. She pulled her reading glasses out of her capacious pocket and planted them on her nose. She would check every electrical device in the place to make sure they didn't have to call the fire department again.

She began with the countertop appliances: toaster, coffeemaker, and electric teakettle, all fine. Then came the larger items.

She'd never fully appreciated how many electrical outlets there were. Cottie had planned well when she'd helped design the associate houses. The rooms were spacious and comfortable, and had more than enough spots for lamps and electronic gear. Everything had been easy to adapt when personal computers became the norm.

Aura Lee pushed herself off the floor and shoved the bookcase behind the sofa back against the wall. No problems with the shelf lights there. She was deciding where to check next when she caught something moving from the corner of her eye. She whirled in time to see a blur speed through the door to the kitchen. Was it a mouse?

Aura Lee didn't like mice. She strode into the kitchen, intent on catching it. Something fluttered at the edge of the refrigerator and she hurried to grab the broom hanging in the pantry. She used it to poke behind the fridge, pushing along the bottom, trying to drive the creature out into the open. Focused on her prey, she didn't see the shadow oozing from behind the appliance, sliding across the floor.

Hearing a sharp cry from the living room she dropped the broom. As she left the kitchen, she saw a gray mist floating toward the stairs. "By the Goddess." The temperature dropped again, becoming unbearably cold.

From the stairwell came another muffled cry.

Kerry.

Aura Lee ran to the steps and had made it up the first three when she encountered an even deeper cold. Suddenly she was blind with it, turned to stone by it, deaf from it. *Death.*

It sank into her, stunning her, stealing her breath.

As she lost consciousness her last thought was,

Cottie, no.

The world went dark.

"Hell's teeth, Max. What's going on in this place?"

Aura Lee's eyelids fluttered. What was Neal doing here? Where was here? She felt a hand on her forehead and reveled in its warmth.

"If I could explain it, I would." Max's voice was sharp with worry. "Kerry, wake up. Come on, luv, make an effort."

A bird trilled with joyous abandon until a motorcycle roared nearby. Aura Lee grimaced at the noise and moved her head from side to side.

"She's coming out of it." Neal picked up one of her hands and patted it. "You're okay, Aura Lee. Open your eyes for me, sweetheart."

"We need to find out what went on in there," Max said roughly. "If I can't get Kerry to surface soon, I'm taking her to hospital."

"She can stay in Brenna's room," Aura Lee whispered.

"That's my girl." Neal dropped a kiss on her cheek and slid his arm under her shoulders, slowly bringing her to a sitting position. The blanket over her slid down and was quickly replaced. Aura Lee opened her eyes and saw they were outside in the courtyard at the base of the associate house stairs. She could see the tree branches swaying in the breeze.

Neil pulled her closer. "Lean against me. I'll hold you up."

Max was nearby, kneeling beside Kerry.

"Is she all right?" Aura Lee looked up into Neal's eyes. "She was in the stairwell longer than I was. It was so cold."

Neal glanced at Max. "Did you hear her?"

"Yes." Max pulled the covers up around Kerry's chin and lay down next to her, holding her close. "Wake up, Kerry. Wake *up.*"

"What happened in there?" Neal asked. "Why did you go inside, anyway?"

The clouds shifted overhead, letting sunshine through, and Aura Lee closed her eyes against the brightness. Her head hurt. "Trying to figure out what happened to Brenna." She sighed. "Stupid, I guess."

"No, not stupid." Neal hugged her. "But it was dangerous. I think it's time to give our ghostly visitors wide berth." He looked over at Max. "Any sign she's coming to?"

"Possibly." Max met his eyes grimly. "She's so cold, I'm having difficulties warming her up. I'm not about to take her back in there." He jerked his head toward the associate house. "Shall we try to get them into the main house?"

"Yeah." Neal looked down at Aura Lee. "What d'you say? Shall we get you back to your place?"

She nodded. "I can walk."

"And deprive me of the chance to do the heroic bit? Sweep you up in my manly arms and remove you from peril? Perish the thought." He grinned at her shaky giggle and pushed himself to his knees. As he began to hoist her up, Rose's pickup came through the gate and stopped near the fountain.

Andrea and Rose spilled from the truck and ran to them as Brenna followed slowly behind. "What's happened now?" demanded Rose.

Andrea raised her brows at Neal and he nodded. With a relieved smile she bent beside Kerry. "What is it, Max?"

"I found them both cold as death in the stairwell. I dragged them out and called Neal, since his number was first on the list." Emotion was thick in his voice.

"We've been trying to get Kerry awake."

"He's in love with her," Aura Lee whispered to Neal. He nodded and winked.

Andrea patted Max's arm in sympathy. "I'm sure she'll be fine. Were you going to take them inside?"

"The main house."

Brenna sat down on the cobblestones beside Aura Lee. "You were in my place?"

Aura Lee reached for her hand and clung to it. "You're going to want to stay with us tonight."

Brenna just sat there. She was sallow, her eyes clouded with fear. "What did you find?"

"We can talk about it later." Aura Lee extended her other hand to Neal. "Why don't the two of you haul me off these bricks. If you'll let me lean a little, you won't have be all heroic, Neal."

"No glory for me." Neal took her by the arm and, with Brenna's help, got her to her feet. "Let's take it really slow."

"Don't worry." Aura Lee felt as if she might sink into the ground. "I won't run ahead."

Rose was holding Kerry's hand tightly and chanting in a low voice near her ear. "Come back to us, Kerry. We need your help. Max is waiting." After a moment, her eyelids moved and she took a sharp breath. "That's it, breathe, Kerry. Breathe deeply."

Soon Kerry was inhaling and exhaling with more regularity. She opened her eyes easily and looked up into Max's face. "Hello."

Max cupped her cheek and bent to kiss her. "Hello." His voice trembled. "You frightened the bejesus out of me."

"Sorry." Kerry's eyes closed again. "Did you find the gloppy stuff?" She began to shiver, her body vibrating as it attempted to restore heat to her, life to her.

Rose frowned at her. "What are you talking about?"

Kerry sighed. "I left it on the foyer table, in a little bag. Aura Lee found it on the couch." She breathed evenly for a while, the shivering dying down, a tiny smile curving her lips.

"I think she's asleep." Rose got to her feet. "I'm too old for this, any of it." She looked toward the main house where Neal and Brenna were guiding Aura Lee up the steps to the porch. She turned back to Max. "You know anything about the bag she mentioned?"

He shook his head. "I'll go see if it's there. Then we'll take her inside." He pushed a few strands of her hair behind her ear and stood up.

As Rose gathered up blankets, Max ran into the associate house and came out a minute later, plastic bag in hand.

"How is it in there?"

Max grimaced. "Nothing jumped out at me, but it feels quite odd. The air is crackling with electricity." He glanced down at the bag.

"What is it?"

Max frowned at it and shook his head slowly. "I can't say for certain, but an unpleasant thought comes to mind."

Rose waited. "And?" she finally prompted him.

"As insane as it might sound, I think it might be ectoplasm."

At his feet Kerry opened her eyes and looked up at him with a sneer. "Ectoplasm? Are you nuts?"

"But, Kerry…"

"I could never be with a man who believes in ectoplasm." Her eyes closed and she was asleep once more.

"If she's arguing, she's getting stronger," Rose said. "Let's get moving."

CHAPTER 25

"Everything I've ever read says that ectoplasm is at best a fiction, and at worst, a fraud. Those damned spiritualists used to make the stuff out of gauze and wet cornstarch." Kerry hit the coffee table with her fist. "I won't let you ruin your reputation claiming anything else."

"Darling," Max said, his voice rough with fatigue. "I won't bandy about the word and my reputation will be fine. I'm the leading authority on hauntings in both the UK and America. A discussion about ectoplasm won't change that."

Noreen groaned and tugged at her hair in frustration. "I realize I missed much of the drama this afternoon, but what does it matter if there *was* ectoplasm on Brenna's couch?"

"*If* that's what it is," Max said with waning patience, "it's enormously important from a scientific point of view."

Kerry snorted. "Scientific? How would you even begin to identify it?"

Max glared at her and she all but snarled at him.

Rose sighed. The day had lasted forever, what with

Aura Lee, Kerry, and Brenna filling the category of walking wounded after their experiences with whatever was turning Brenna's apartment into a deep freeze. The night ahead promised to be longer still and more contentious if the current conversation was any indication. If she added the possibility of further paranormal events, she was ready to check into a shiny new, never-been-haunted motel, or perhaps an expensive mental institution.

They'd gathered for a makeshift snack, choosing the living room for its fireplace warmth. Paper plates held the remains of cheese and crackers, and inroads had been made into the wine and spirits. They'd focused on creature comforts and, for the most part, fitful conversation. The atmosphere thrummed with tension, fear, and fatigue. Everyone was on edge.

"Stop arguing," Rose ordered loudly. Silence descended on the room as they all stared at her in surprise.

"We have to pool our resources and compare notes on what's gone on today. Ectoplasm is at the end of the list."

Noreen eyed her with respect. "You've got the makings of a head mistress in you, Rose. Well done."

"Thank you." Rose waved a hand at the meal's debris. "Let's clear up this mess and get a laptop or two fired up." She glanced at the mantel clock. "We'll regroup in fifteen minutes and sort through what happened today. Agreed?"

"Sure." Kerry reached for paper plates.

"Yeah." Andrea stood up and grabbed at napkins and silverware.

"I'll help with the glasses." Brenna took several as she pushed herself up from the floor.

Rose turned to Aura Lee as she started to rise. "Let everyone else do the work. Unless you need the bathroom, I'd suggest you hold onto your piece of the sofa and put up your feet."

"That sounds good." Aura Lee leaned against the sofa back and nestled into the blanket around her. "I don't know if I'll ever get warm again." Her face lit with an idea. "I know! We could make hot toddies. Wouldn't that be good?"

"Sounds great—and I'll make them. Kerry can help me." Rose put on her best frown. "Seriously, don't move. I'll fill up the samovar and we can each get our own. Okay?"

Aura Lee had again sunk back into the cushions. "Okay. Thanks."

"You're welcome. Noreen, will you stay here with her?" When Noreen looked askance, Rose explained. "Nobody is left alone tonight. We stick to pairs or more. I don't want anybody else to be vulnerable to the deep freeze."

Noreen nodded and watched Rose scoop up a couple of paper plates and go into the kitchen. "She's really got the bit between her teeth tonight, doesn't she?"

"We scared her. We scared *me*."

Noreen was silent for a moment. Finally she asked, "What happened at Brenna's?"

Aura Lee shivered under her blanket. "Something was in there. Something that produced the most soul-leeching cold I've ever felt." She looked blindly at her feet, propped on the coffee table. "I thought I would die from that cold."

"Oh, my dear." Noreen clasped her hand comfortingly. "I'm sorry you went through that. I've been frightened lately, but not from anything nearly as terrifying as that."

"I'm glad you haven't been." Aura Lee let out a sigh. "Rose is right. We need to put our heads together and puzzle out what's causing these terrible things, why they're happening. How else will we be able stay here?"

Before long Andrea came back into the room carrying a polished silver samovar etched with flowers. She set it on the sideboard and lit the candle resting under it. "You'll love this, Aura Lee," she said with forced cheer. "Lots of spices, lots of rum. It'll warm you right up."

Kerry eased past her with a tray of glasses and a pitcher of water and arranged them on the bar table. Max followed with mugs for the toddies and when he'd stacked them near the samovar, he reclaimed his seat.

When the doorbell pealed the smile slipped from Andrea's face. "Who could this—oh, it's probably Neal." She started to leave the room but Noreen stopped her.

"We have a new rule. The buddy system is in effect for everything. Nobody is to wander off alone."

Max stood up. "It's a good plan. I'll go with you."

Andrea blinked and nodded. As Brenna carted in a tray of cookies and pastries, she and Max went together to answer the door.

Aura Lee noted how carefully Brenna placed the tray on the coffee table. The shadows under her eyes had grown larger since that morning. "How are you feeling, dear?"

Brenna's smile didn't reach her eyes. "Like Janet Leigh in the *Psycho* shower scene. Somebody's going to reach around that shower curtain any minute now. How are *you* feeling?"

When Aura Lee just shook her head, Brenna nodded. "Yeah." She jerked toward a sound from the door and relaxed when Rose carried Strudel into the room and set her on Aura Lee's lap.

Max came in from the hallway, Neal and Andrea trailing behind him hand in hand. Neal greeted Rose with a kiss on the cheek, and waited as Andrea curled up on the sofa, sitting beside her. Brenna grabbed a blanket and sat on the floor.

Rose slid a piece of paper from the table and glanced at it. "I would love for us to call it a night, but we have to go over what happened this afternoon at Brenna's place. Our spirit or spirits are becoming more aggressive." Her gray eyes were dark with trouble. "If there's anything we can do to bring this danger to an end, we've got to find it. Brenna, you go first. You went for the camera and the book. Do you remember what happened while you were there?"

Brenna nodded. "I'm not likely to forget it. In a nutshell, I got the book and started upstairs for the camera. My cell rang when I got to the top of the stairs—it was Dink—and all of a sudden I could smell my grandmother's perfume. It was so strong, so reminiscent of her—I just lost it. I think I started back down the stairs, but I'm not sure. Nothing else is clear in my mind except seeing you bending over me. I was lying on the floor."

"Did you feel that awful cold?" Kerry asked.

Brenna frowned, considering, and shook her head slowly. "I don't think so. It was the scent of Wind Song that did me in. Gran always called it her signature scent."

"Aromas can trigger such visceral responses," Kerry said. "They activate the primitive brain."

"Have you smelled this Wind Song before?" Max asked. "Whilst you've been here at Wisdom Court, I mean?"

"No, not that I'm aware of." Brenna rubbed one brow, thinking back. "I've been dreaming about her nearly every night ever since I arrived. The dreams have been hard to take, really scary, but I don't think any of them involved scent."

Noreen looked up from the tablet where she'd been entering notes. "Were you frightened when you smelled the perfume? Did you have any sense of another presence?"

"Yeah, I kind of did." Brenna's eyes narrowed as she thought. "I remember thinking something was...*off* when I looked for the book in the screening room. It was one of those thoughts in passing. I wanted to get out of there, so I didn't follow up on it."

"Why is that?" Max asked in a quiet voice. "What made you feel that way?"

She shrugged. "I was spooked when I got there. I've been nervous ever since the other night, when the sounds went all wonky. But today the rooms felt almost...electrical. The air was tight, you know?"

They were silent, taken aback. Finally Rose let out a breath. "In some ways that's the scariest thing I've heard today."

"Yes, although the competition is getting fierce." Noreen typed for another moment. "Let's break out the toddies and then it'll be Aura Lee's turn."

"Back to the baked goods." Andrea took several cookies and pastries, handing the plate to Neal. "I don't know if the sugar chemically helps or not, but I do find comfort in it."

"Maybe because it's real," Neal said around a bite of cherry Danish. "It's physical...sensory. Of this world."

Aura Lee's smile slipped. "Yes, it is." Strudel put her paw on Aura Lee's leg, taking a morsel of cookie when she held it out to her.

They served themselves the refreshments, and as the brief stir of activity diminished, Aura Lee cleared her throat. "Before you ask *me* anything, I have a question for Brenna. Why did you put Christmas paper on the kitchen windows?"

Brenna was surprised into a laugh. "My secret's out. I kept getting the creeps from the dark windows at night. It felt like somebody was looking in at me. And I meant to ask about curtains," she added, "but so much was going on, I just forgot. I hunted around and found wrapping paper in the pantry." She smiled at Aura Lee. "It helps."

"I'm glad of that. Dolores loved having the windows uncovered so she could look for deer in the mornings." Aura Lee lifted her shoulders in a what-can-you-do movement. "I'll have to start asking associates what they prefer."

"If we have any more," Rose said softly. No one said anything, and she added, "I honestly don't know if we can allow anyone new to come here. For all the welcome *we* give, our invisible residents aren't particularly friendly."

"No crepe-hanging yet," Max said confidently. "Let's keep trying to make sense of what happened. Aura Lee."

She took a deep breath. "Kerry and I went into Brenna's apartment and we were paying attention to smells, too, since we'd called the fire department about smoke. We both smelled ozone, or something like it. I looked for frayed wires on the appliances and checked the electric cords in the living room. The ecto—" She glanced at Rose. "We found the jelly-like substance on the leather couch and put it in a plastic bag. Wait, we did that first," she added quickly. "I did the wire hunt after that. I saw something moving in the kitchen, on the floor. I thought it was a mouse and went after it with the broom, but when it got to the living room, it looked more like a little cloud, like mist." Her voice trembled and Strudel made a whining sound. "It went up the stairs and I started to follow. I got caught by the cold," she said simply. "It took me over completely and for a moment I thought Cottie had come for me. That's all I can remember."

Noreen finished entering a line on her tablet and peered up from the screen. "So Brenna didn't feel the cold but you did. That's puzzling."

Max nodded. "Yes. I'd much rather have consistent accounts. Sometimes it makes it easier to figure out what the spirits are after. Now, you, luv," he said to Kerry.

The adventures of the day had taken a toll, her pale skin and shadow-smudged eyes giving her an air of fragility. "I started up the stairs to the bedroom. The light was out, and the switch didn't work. The higher I went, the darker it got. Then I heard something." She thought for a moment. "Bumps, like steps or something dropped. It freaked me out a little. I felt the cold then. It just...enveloped me, soaked into me. I couldn't move because of it." She took a shaky breath. "The only other thing I can remember happened right before that. I looked behind me for some reason, down the stairs. It stretched back like a tunnel, like I was looking through the wrong end of a telescope. It was weird." Max tightened his arm around her shoulders and she rested her head against him.

"All right," muttered Noreen, typing efficiently. "Another encounter with the cold."

"*Why* so much cold, do you think?" Rose looked at Max. "It keeps recurring."

"It's one of the more common phenomena in hauntings. The prevailing theory is that ghosts drain the energy around them in their efforts to materialize." He reached for his cup and took a swallow. "Living people feel the drop in temperature and usually assume it's an indication of a spirit presence. What's different about what you've experienced here is the extremity of the cold. I've encountered drops of ten, maybe twelve degrees, as measured by infrared thermometers. What you've described are much more severe. You, my sweet," he said lightly to Kerry, "were almost as cold as a North Sea herring."

"But not me." Brenna rubbed her arms and Rose tossed her a throw. "Thanks. I'm chilly now, but at the time it was all about Gran's perfume. I wish I had some idea of why these things keep happening." She huddled under the warm material.

Max stood up and took his mug and Kerry's for refills. "What if your grandmother is trying to contact you? Can you think of a reason she might do that?"

"No way." Brenna's face had become blank. "By the time she died she was totally gone. Alzheimer's disease," she added when Max looked bewildered. "How could she possibly haunt me if she didn't remember who *she* was..." Her voice wobbled. "Let alone me."

"Oh, my dear," Rose began, but the doorbell rang loudly. "Who on earth could that be?" she asked over Strudel's barking.

"I'll go see." Andrea got to her feet.

"Take Neal with you," Aura Lee and Noreen chimed in unison.

Andrea held out her hand and Neal let her pull him up. He said something to her as they left the room and she laughed softly.

"You do realize," Max said gently to Brenna, "one doesn't necessarily retain in the afterlife the condition one died from."

Pain flashed in her eyes. "How can you possibly know? Have ghosts told you that?"

Before Max could answer, Andrea came back, Neal behind her with another man.

"Who's this?" Rose asked.

Brenna turned to glance behind her. When she saw the tall, shaggy-haired figure she cried, "Dink!" Scrambling to her feet she struggled to unwrap herself from the throw. "You're here."

"Brenna." He strode to her and grabbed her by one hand. In an instant he'd pulled her into his arms and she was clutching him to her. He held her tightly and shot a challenging look at them over her head. "What the hell is going on here?"

CHAPTER 26

Rose came down the stairs slowly, vaguely aware of a floating sensation, holding the rail just in case she discovered she was too tired to walk the rest of the way. She sighed inwardly. It had been an exceedingly long day.

Brenna tried to regain control after Dink's arrival, but she'd reached her breaking point. She clung to him, tears trailing down her cheeks, content just to be in his arms. When she ran out of tears she asked him why he'd come. "How could you even afford the plane ticket?"

"I knew I had to do something." Dink was clearly anxious. "One minute you were talking to me and you sounded so out of it. Next thing I knew you were gone and I couldn't tell if you just put down the phone or if something happened to you. I kept trying to call you back but all I got were weird noises on the cell." He pulled her tighter to him. "I was scared for you, Bren." She stroked his cheek.

"I told Sandoval—he's the new manager—about it, and that I was taking the first plane I could get to Denver. He was great. He ran me home and waited while I got my credit card out of the freezer and grabbed some clothes. He even gave me a ride to the airport."

"It must've cost the earth." Brenna eyes were filling again.

"That's what an emergency fund is for," Dink said firmly. "I had to make sure you're all right." Brenna leaned her head against his chest and they held onto each other for a long time.

Rose asked Andrea if the two could use her room, and changed the sheets, escorting them up the stairs when it was ready. "Andrea will stay with Neal," she assured them. "Get some sleep and we'll talk tomorrow." Brenna clasped her hand, nodding her thanks, and closed the door.

When she arrived downstairs Rose found the others still sitting in the living room. "I thought sure you'd have gone to bed by now."

Andrea shook her head. "I, for one, am counting on our figuring out some things tonight. Not that I blame Brenna for fading. This was one horrible day for her. Is she okay?"

"I think so." Rose put a hand over her mouth to smother her yawn. "Having Dink here helps a lot."

Noreen frowned down at her tablet. "I've been reorganizing my notes, and I have a couple of things to talk over with you."

Max came in from the kitchen bearing a tray of steaming cups. "I made coffee. Toddies won't get us much farther in our research."

"He makes great coffee." Kerry took a cup and smiled at him.

"Good man." Neal helped hand out the mugs and took a long swallow of the hot brew. "Okay, I'm ready if you are."

"I made a command decision to forget about

Caldicott's journal, at least for now," began Noreen. "The more I tried to factor in crazed Nazi sympathizers and Gypsy protection spells, the more confused I became. As a result I've concentrated on the events of the last week or so. Basically it's the time Brenna's been here." She sniffed and dabbed her nose with a tissue. "Blasted tree dust." She stuffed the tissue in her pocket. "As before, following Andrea's arrival, the paranormal activity has increased each day since Brenna came last week." Her smile was pointed. "Don't you find that interesting?"

Rose sank into her chair. "I find any paranormal activity interesting, when I'm not terrified by it. But why would Brenna's being here be a cause of the increase?"

"That is the question, isn't it?" Noreen peered at Rose over her glasses. "With Andrea, it was artistic ability combined with her intuiting skill as a forensic artist that enabled her to channel Kelvin Haslett. I think it was Aura Lee who recognized the causal effect Andrea had just by coming here."

"Tell me more." Max stood beside them, craning to read the screen. "This might lead to something."

Noreen nodded an acknowledgement. "Brenna is a filmmaker, and while she's taken a couple of photos of the face in the attic window, that alone hasn't told us much. I asked myself, though, what did she bring with her besides her talent?" She moved her questioning gaze over them one by one. When she saw recognition move across Andrea's face, she smiled.

"Her grief," Andrea murmured. "She's so sad about her grandmother she can hardly stand it. Everything is colored by her sorrow."

Noreen nodded. "It's like a lens for one of her cameras. And she's told us several times about her dreams. What if those dreams represent more than just her subconscious working through that grief?"

Max moved back to share Kerry's chair. She scooted over on the cushion to allow him enough room. "You're suggesting that the haunting activity is tailored to specific people here at Wisdom Court?"

"Remember how I began sensing Cottie's desire to communicate with me after she died?" Aura Lee cut in, a hopeful light in her eyes. "I was certain she had something to tell me. I still feel that way. If I'd just been able to control my fear, maybe I'd know what it was."

"All right, this is good." Max pulled his notebook off the coffee table and was rapidly scribbling across one page. "Let's say Brenna is a receiver because of her grandmother's death. Aura Lee's one because of Ms. Wyntham's death. Now, in those cases, it could be the personal contact that allows the barrier between the here and now and the Other Side to be breached." He looked up from the page. "What about Rose and the discovery of Ms. Wyntham's journal? And the fragment of the title page Kerry found?"

Noreen shrugged. "As I said, I've tabled Caldicott's journal for now. Kerry had minor brushes with the things she saw on the mountain when we discovered what happened to Kelvin. But she did find that fragment this week, and today she and Aura Lee were affected by whatever caused that terrible cold. Earlier this week Rose felt the icy chill when she was led to the journal. It might be a stretch, but what if that cold is simply a by-product of an entity trying to give us information?"

"Cottie?" Aura Lee blinked against tears. She looked at Max. "Do you think it could be Cottie?"

He was frowning at his notes, but at the plea in her voice he nodded. "It could be. Perhaps she's shaky on controlling the impact she has on her surroundings."

Aura Lee clasped her hands together. "That would be so wonderful!"

"You appear unconvinced, Rose." Max glanced back down at the notebook.

Rose fought off another yawn. "I don't see a connection between the cold and my circle of fountain rocks, or our dinner rearranged around the floral centerpiece. I see too many variables for a cohesive theory."

Max glanced at the woman beside him. "Kerry?"

She was silent for a bit. "I don't know," she said finally. "Yesterday I would've been a lot more skeptical than I am today. It's possible, Noreen, but you haven't mentioned the hand reaching through Aura Lee's tray, or the business with Brenna's stars."

Andrea sat up straighter. "*I* have a theory about those stars. It hit me after Brenna told me about her grandmother. Poor kid," she added in a mutter. "Anyway, she said her Gran was always telling her she—Brenna—would be a star someday with her photography. What if those stars Brenna saw on her film were like a message from Gran? You know, *I always said you'd be a star, here are all these stars so you know who's trying to tell you something.*"

Noreen's eyes narrowed as she considered the idea. "*At times a course is found by those acting in concert; needed is the vision to see the way within the tangled strands.*' Caterina Milsap, 1801 to 1852." She nodded. "Your theory is possibly inspired, my dear."

"It's a good idea." Neal kissed her soundly on the cheek.

"What I keep wondering," said Kerry, "is why that sort of warm-fuzzy is happening on the one hand, but we still have the actively dangerous arctic chill on the other." She scowled. "If there are several spirits behind these manifestations, wouldn't you think they could compare notes about the special effects? Share the technology?"

Her voice was so snarky, Rose laughed in spite of herself. "I don't know what it's like on the so-called Other Side, but maybe they don't interact. Maybe they're in separate dimensions, divided from each other."

"No." Aura Lee shook her head stubbornly. "I don't like that idea at all. What's the point of being a ghost if you can't have company doing it?"

"I think we've agreed on the notion of our ghosts trying to tell us something." Noreen pressed at the spot between her brows. "After reading her journal, I believe Caldicott wants us to know more about her life and the history of Wisdom Court, to say nothing of the talisman."

"And maybe Gran can't leave while Brenna is still so upset," Andrea offered.

"Those are comforting ideas," Kerry said. "But some of what we've learned about Caldicott's early life at least suggests we might also be dealing with more sinister forces. I can't help but wonder if Wisdom Court has already been traced because of the talisman. If it exists, and if it's here, we'd be up the creek if it were signaling somehow to the bad guys. In that scenario, some of our manifestations might be the ghosts of those who were planning to subvert the war efforts, for instance."

Max groaned. "Leave it to you to pooh-pooh the supernatural and then come up with the most frightening possibilities yet."

"You've got that right." Rose reached into the nearby basket for a blanket. "I'm getting cold. Let's turn up the flames." As soon as the words were out of her mouth she looked at Max in dismay. "You don't think—"

Andrea shuddered, twisting round in her chair. "Did you see that?"

"What?"

"A shadow, it went toward the window."

They all craned to see. "I don't see anything," Aura Lee began and stopped. "There—isn't there a grayness near the striped chair. Look, it's moving!"

Kerry made a squeaking sound as a flowing shape took on greater clarity. "It's like looking through a shape made of mist," she whispered. "Is it coming toward us?"

"Don't say that." Andrea got up from the chair, grabbing Neal's hand and pulling him up. "Let's get out of here, come on!" She tugged at him.

"Wait." His eyes were fixed on the apparition.

Floating above the rug, the nearly transparent silhouette came forward very slowly. Aura Lee stood up, forcing Strudel to the floor. "Cottie?" she rasped, trembling violently. "Is it you?" Beside her the dog pressed herself to the floor fearfully, whimpering.

Noreen had hold of Rose's hand and was squeezing it tightly. "What do you want?"

"Hush." Max's voice was barely above a whisper. "It's using all its strength to materialize. Just wait. Perhaps it will be able to speak."

They stood, hardly breathing, until Strudel made a sharp little sound and backed, whining, to the door.

The figure floated for a moment more and faded into nothing.

NIGHTMIRROR

———— ◆ ————

Brenna walked down the vacant hallway, light behind her bled to dark.

Each door shut, no knobs to turn, a sly cold swirled at every step.

Empty, empty, nothing left.

Fear pulled her, forced her on through whispers.

You're all alone. Nothing left.

Release your grip. Be no more.

Bitter cold tugged her, dragged her, deepened pain.

Forget and follow, follow us.

"Don't listen, chickie!"

She jerked awake inside the dream, saw nothing, eyes fixed on the end. *Gran?*

A whiff of Wind Song touched her mind, she roused again, saw the glass at hallway's end.

A figure in the mirror waited.

Icy air pushed her closer, dread beside her, toward the reflection.

Echoes built, collided, tore at her ears like ravens after prey.

End the suffering. Be no more.

Stop. Her voice was weak, uncertain.

Give up the fight.

STOP. Sounds crashed around her, unabated.

Brenna stood before the glass and saw the creature, the shell.

Gran? Off-kilter face and grimace-smile?

Come closer, closer.

Evil flicked from Not-Gran's hooded eyes.

NO

The outline wavered, edges hazy.

She hit the glass, saw something scuttle.

Come with us. Come inside.

"Brenna, let me go or they'll steal me."

Gran? She looked, saw wrong shapes shift above a yellow brick road.

She bent, picked up a brick, hard in her hand, and hit the glass—hit the glass—hit the glass.

Crashing, shards flung to both sides, pieces falling all around. She stumbled forward, glass crunching, soles afire.

"Chickie, they'll fight to keep me here. And you."

Her heart skipped and the war in her mind raged. *You were gone, nothing left.*

"I'm whole again. Let me go."

Even in my dreams I'm broken, I can't forget the end of you.

"Don't forget, look inside. I'm with you, always. Life's a movie. Leave them on the cutting room floor."

Them?

"I came to give you stars. They caught me in their cold."

I watched as you were stripped away. Now I'm scared I'll lose me, too.

"Focus on now. They use dread to bind. Their evil

needs your fear and pain."

Evil?

"Old and waiting, searching for it, have to have it. Warn the others."

Why me? Why you?

"Attack the wounded, erode from within. I gave you stars to make the best. Defeat them."

Gran?

"Set me free."

A blast of cold hit swift and hard. She felt Gran twist in a fetid current, her essence nearly gone.

Brenna fell to her knees and shouted. *I set you free! I set you free!*

A mist of Wind Song rose then ebbed. "I love you," whispered on the air.

CHAPTER 27

———— ◆ ————

Dink felt the mattress move beneath him and shifted toward Brenna, a smile forming as he turned. She was already standing beside the bed, taking a step toward the door. "Bren?"

She kept on walking, a slender figure in dark ski pajamas, opened the door, closed it behind her.

"What the hell…" He rolled out of bed and yanked on pants, scooping up a tee shirt as he hurried to follow her. His hand slipped on the doorknob and he realized he was sweating. He shoved the door open. "Bren, what's the deal? Bren?"

She was at the end of the hallway, taking the first step down the stairs.

Dink caught up and followed behind her. "Brenna, what's going on?"

The odors of coffee and waffles floated up from the kitchen and his stomach reminded him how long it had been since he'd eaten. He reached for Brenna's shoulder and touched her. "Honey, what's wrong? Why won't you talk to me?"

She took the last step down and stopped near the table.

Aura Lee turned from the counter, her smile fading as she caught sight of Brenna's face. Her eyes lifted to Dink and she whispered, "She's asleep."

"What?" he demanded and went silent at her shushing sound. He came around to look directly at Brenna. Her face was bone white, her blank eyes staring straight ahead. "She got out of bed and came right down here," he said in a low voice. "Didn't talk to me, didn't even look at me."

Aura Lee bustled to the door and waved one hand in a summoning gesture. "Come here, quick!"

As Rose came into the kitchen, Brenna moved again, her face grimacing in horror. She bumped into Rose but eased past her, somehow moving ahead through the others crowding in. Her eyes were open but looked inward. She lifted one hand to reach ahead, tilting her hand up as if placing her palm against something.

"Oh, my God," Kerry whispered. She groped for Max's arm and hung onto it. "She's sleepwalking." As the words came out of her mouth, Brenna reached forward, barely missing Neal, who had followed Andrea through the door from the dining room.

Neal tugged Andrea to his side and got out of the way as Brenna took more tentative steps, one hand extended in front of her. Then her hand fell to her side and she advanced, faster now, through the dining room, into the foyer.

"Where's she going?" Noreen asked, but no one could answer her.

Brenna went to the front door and stood for a moment, staring into it as if it held secrets only she could see. Her hand fumbled for the knob and turned it back and forth until Max reached over her shoulder and opened it for her.

"Gran," they heard her say. She stepped onto the

porch and went toward the steps.

"You're letting her walk out of here?" Kerry protested.

Max barely glanced at her. "We don't dare try to wake her when she's this deep into whatever state she's in. It's too dangerous."

Brenna murmured, "Stop." A moment later she said it more loudly. "Stop." She stared ahead, unblinking, and walked down the steps to the courtyard, face twisting as if in pain.

"No!" she screamed suddenly, and the others froze in shock. She threw a punch at the air and before they could react she was speeding across the cobblestones toward the fountain.

"Quickly," Rose ordered. "Don't let her hurt herself on the stones."

Neal ran after her, Max close behind, but before they could reach her, she stopped at the wall of the fountain and yanked a rock from its edge. She raised it with both hands and hit the wall, hit the wall, hit the wall and a larger stone fell to the bricks where she stood.

Max bent to pick up the rock and moved it carefully out of the way. Behind him Aura Lee was crying, and both Rose and Noreen had their arms around her. Andrea and Kerry were ashen-faced and trembling.

Brenna stood swaying.

Neal drew closer to her, but before he could touch her, Dink ran past him. As he reached Brenna she fell to her knees, shouting, "I set you free! I set you free!"

Dink knelt beside her and was able to catch her as she slowly toppled sideways to the ground. He gathered her to him, whispering softly, when an engine roared to life and he swiveled around to find the source of the noise.

Rose's pickup, parked beside the main house, jerked

into motion, the tires turning to aim straight for Brenna and Dink. He scooped her into his arms and lurched to the side, falling and rolling with her as the truck plowed into the wall of the fountain with a tremendous crunching sound.

Brenna lay on the cobblestones, covered by Dink's body. Her eyes opened and she looked up at him, and then struggled to get out from under him. He helped her sit up and put one arm around her. "I did it," she said in a breathless voice. "I saved Gran, I set her free."

Neal ran to the truck and forced open the passenger door. He reached across the seat to turn the key and take it out of the ignition. The acrid smell of ozone spilled from the cab.

Water from the fountain reached Brenna's legs and she scrambled to her feet, finally noticing the others grouped around her and Dink. Noreen and Rose still had hold of Aura Lee, and Kerry and Max were walking nearer to the fountain.

"I saved Gran," Brenna said again.

"From what?" Andrea was the worse for wear, leaning against Kerry.

"From *Them*. I don't know who they are, but they were holding her prisoner. She said they trapped her in their cold."

"What?" Max said sharply.

Kerry shuddered. "We know about that, don't we?" she said to Aura Lee. The older woman nodded wanly.

Tears trailed down Brenna's cheeks. "Gran said they're hunting for *it*, that they have to have *it*." She wiped her face with both hands. "They're evil and they're coming for us."

Neal came around the pickup, keys in hand. "The keys were in the ignition."

Noreen's wise eyes met Max's troubled gaze. "*It.* Could it be the talisman? Could it be that insanely simple?"

"Simple?" Kerry's voice cracked on the word. "Nothing about any of this is simple. What in the world are we going to do?"

Rose took several steps toward the fountain and gingerly sat on an undamaged portion of its wall. "In a minute we'll go turn off the fountain pump." She looked at the pickup, frowning, and then met Neal's eyes. "I never leave the keys in the ignition."

Neal nodded and turned his head to the fountain wall. "That stone she pulled out was cemented in. I checked the mortar last week."

Brenna pulled away from Dink to walk around the pickup, staring at the crumpled fender, sloshing through the growing pool of water spreading across the cobblestones. As she came round the box of the truck, a shaft of sun reflected off something metallic at the fountain's edge. "Hey, look at this." She shoved a few rocks off what appeared to be a strong box and pulled on the handle. It was wedged against a piece of the wall and didn't move. "A little help here?"

Dink came to her side and pushed aside the pile of stones and bricks. Brenna gripped the handle and lifted the box out of the water.

"You want me to carry it?" Dink asked.

"It's not very heavy." Brenna took it to a dryer spot but as she lowered it to the cobblestones, she lost her hold on the wet handle and dropped the box, the lid snapping open.

Inside it was a book. In gold letters the title shone in the sunlight. *My Personal Journal: 1946 to 1955.*

"By the Goddess." Aura Lee's gazed moved over the trashed pickup, the broken fountain, her friends in varying degrees of shock. "Another of Cottie's journals." She looked at the water spreading further and started to laugh.

"What is it?" Neal came to her side and put his arm around her shoulders. Aura Lee laughed even harder, turning to rest her forehead against his shoulder.

"Is she hysterical?" he asked Rose.

"Cottie kept trying." Aura Lee gurgled. "I told you she was trying! All those rocks from Rose's fountains—time after time she took them out. Over and over again she put them in circles. She kept recreating the circular fountain, and all the time her journal was hidden in the courtyard fountain." Aura Lee wiped tears off her cheeks and laughed some more.

"Didn't I tell you?" she challenged Rose. "Didn't I say it was a message for us all along?" She took a step toward the fountain and nearly tripped. Neal grabbed her arm and helped her to the wall where Rose was sitting, easing her down beside her.

Taking Rose's hand, Aura Lee looked up at the sky and called cheerfully, "Hello, Cottie! We're listening now!"

Turn the page for an

excerpt from

ALL
IN
BAD TIME

The Wisdom Court Series
Book Three

Yvonne Montgomery

"Evie, wake up."

The woman asleep on the narrow futon stirred, her hair golden strands in the moonlight shining through the gap between the window curtains. Her eyelids trembled, then stilled as her breath sighed out through pale lips and she settled into the pillow, one hand curled beside her cheek.

The silence thickened in the small room, grew heavy, and the air chilled. A scraping from the bookshelves against the wall started—stopped— started once more. The woman on the futon frowned and turned her head toward the sound but slept on.

"Evie, wake up."

The rasping whisper broke through the grip sleep had on her mind and Eve Stewart opened her eyes. Light flashed from the surface of her computer monitor and she jerked to a sitting position, her breath caught in her throat. "Who's there?" she whispered.

She waited, gaze darting from the window to the door, back to the computer. The hush pressed against her ears as she swiveled her head to look toward the closet. She braced herself on the hard mattress and tried to shift her legs over the edge of the bed, but the pain in her left knee pushed a groan out of her and she waited for the sharp ache to subside. She hunched her shoulders against the cold air.

"There's no one here," Eve growled to herself. "There's never anyone here." Ever since the accident she'd been plagued by strange fears and hazy memories she couldn't bring into focus.

The last four nights, though, had replayed the same scenario as tonight—the abrupt awakening, always with a sense of another's presence in the room. And a helpless feeling of dread followed by a growing anger. Was someone playing tricks on her? Was her sister's oddball boyfriend as sick of her living with them as she was of being there? Had he decided to freak her out so she'd leave for good?

Paranoid much?

The thought came out of nowhere and she almost smiled. A frown quickly drew her brows together. That had been happening a fair amount as well, the differences in her internal conversations. *All writers talk to themselves,* she told herself for the hundredth time. *Not all of them wake up one day with a new voice inside their heads*, she answered herself.

Maybe we're schizophrenic.

"God!" Eve slid off the futon, hand reaching to brace her knee, and lurched away from the bed. Had she *heard* that or was it just in her head? "What the hell is happening to me?"

She limped toward the computer and reached the desk chair, sitting down hard, wincing as her leg throbbed again. Her breathing was fast, as if she'd been running. "I've got to get out of here," she whispered.

She waited for the pain to ease and tried to work through this latest fear. As she made her way back to the futon she started a list of things to do. She would sleep and tomorrow would be manageable. Lindsey had agreed to let her stay until she could get around a little better. When that glorious day arrived, she would leave for Wisdom Court.

"I'll start packing my books tomorrow," she murmured as she tried to get comfortable on the futon. She moved her head back and forth to indent the pillow. "That'll make me feel ready."

Her eyes closed and she deliberately slowed her breathing. As she sank toward the lazy feeling in her head that presaged sleep, she yawned and pulled the covers up to her chin. *It'll all work out.* Soon her breathing was even.

"Evie, wake up."

She gasped and jackknifed up, looking around wildly. And she clearly heard the raspy voice say, "He's coming for you."

ALL IN BAD TIME

available in print and ebook

THE
WISDOM COURT
SERIES

Yvonne Montgomery became afraid of the dark, after her parents allowed her to see Psycho at the tender age of twelve.

Now Yvonne lives in a shadowy three-story Victorian house in Denver's historic Capitol Hill where her imagination rises to the challenge when the old floor-boards creak for no reason and the window panes rattle without wind.